CU00405480

Praise for *The Art of Killing Well*

"A visually rich, witty variation on the big-house-murder theme . . . A stylish book, ironic and fast-moving, a novel with which to have fun. Anyone seeking the definitive summer read, complete with several recipes, need look no further"

EILEEN BATTERSBY, *Irish Times*

"Like a cross between *The Hundred Year Old Man Who Climbed Out of the Window and Disappeared* and the slyest, cleverest of Christie novels, *The Art of Killing Well* is one of those rare books that will keep you grinning from beginning to end" *Sunday Herald*

"Ideal holiday reading, funny, compelling, unpredictable and immensely satisfying" *Irish Examiner*

"With its tongue-in-cheek wit and lively characterisation, Malvaldi's novel is a delight to read . . . He has created an entertaining tale that holds the reader's attention but never takes itself too seriously"

NICK RENNISON, *BBC History*

"Malvaldi has cooked up a gentle, atmospheric Agatha Christie-esque number with plenty of tongue-in-cheek wit and period detail in a mystery that finishes with a cute and clever twist . . . A tasty Michelin three-star book" *Weekend Sport*

"[An] intelligent, gentle and atmospheric story that will keep you smiling from start to finish. Malvaldi's always tongue-in-cheek and occasionally downright sly depiction of a crumbling nobility struggling to come to terms with the changes nationhood has brought is absolutely magnificent." *Crime Review*

Also by Marco Malvaldi in English translation
Game for Five
Three-card Monte
The Measure of a Man

The Pellegrino Artusi Mysteries:
The Art of Killing Well

102   23-23   £4.00

Marco Malvaldi

FOUL DEEDS AND
FINE DYING

Translated from the Italian by
Howard Curtis

MACLEHOSE PRESS
QUERCUS · LONDON

First published in the Italian language as *Il borghese Pellegrino*
by Sellerio Editore, 2020
First published in Great Britain in 2023 by

MacLehose Press
An imprint of Quercus Publishing Ltd
Carmelite House
50 Victoria Embankment
London EC4Y 0DZ

An Hachette UK company

Copyright © 2020 Sellerio Editore, Palermo
English translation copyright © 2023 by Howard Curtis

The moral right of Marco Malvaldi to be identified
as the author of this work has been asserted in accordance with
the Copyright, Designs and Patents Act, 1988.

Howard Curtis asserts their moral right to be identified
as the translator of the work.

This book has been translated thanks to a translation grant awarded by
the Italian Ministry of Foreign Affairs and International Cooperation.

*Questo libro è stato tradotto grazie a un contributo alla traduzione assegnato
dal Ministero degli Affari Esteri e della Cooperazione Internazionale italiano.*

All rights reserved. No part of this publication may be reproduced
or transmitted in any form or by any means, electronic or mechanical,
including photocopy, recording, or any information storage and retrieval
system, without permission in writing from the publisher.

A CIP catalogue record for this book is available from the British Library.

ISBN (HB) 978 1 52941 538 4
ISBN (Ebook) 978 1 52941 540 7

This book is a work of fiction. Names, characters, businesses,
organisations, places and events are either the product of the author's
imagination or are used fictitiously. Any resemblance to actual persons,
living or dead, events or locales is entirely coincidental.

Designed and typeset in Miller by Libanus Press Ltd
Printed and bound in Great Britain by Clays Ltd, Elcograf S.p.A.

Papers used by MacLehose Press are from well-managed forests and
other responsible sources.

To Cinzia, who trusted in me

The average piece of junk is probably more meaningful
than our criticism designating it so.
ANTON EGO, *Ratatouille*

Beginning

"The phenomenon that is the subject of today's lecture is a phenomenon so complex that to analyse it wearies the mind and discourages scientific enquiry."

The lecture hall is packed to the rafters, standing room only, and yet, apart from the sound made by the heels of the man walking up and down in front of the desk, not the slightest noise can be heard.

"Nevertheless, as we will show, even within such an intricate phenomenon, a phenomenon that cannot be grasped by the intellect, it is possible to find a number of immutable facts."

The lack of noise may perhaps be explained by the disparate nature of the audience attending the lecture. It is a well-known fact that the degree of noise in any kind of gathering is often in direct relation to how well those attending know one another. A class of some twenty students makes much more commotion than the same number of people in an orthopaedist's waiting room. And in this case the listeners are distinctly varied.

"And the first fact that we must accept, and which will guide us in today's investigation, is that the trajectory traced by this phenomenon is not a straight line but rather a parabola."

Listeners who have nothing in common apart from their admiration for the Honourable Paolo Mantegazza, Senator of the Kingdom, Professor of Physiology at the University of Florence and author of a great number of books on the most diverse subjects.

There are a considerable number of ladies of all ages, more

than one with intense blushes on their faces. This is because Professore Mantegazza's books on the physiology of pleasure, especially female pleasure, are well known, as are his public lectures on the subject. There are many who say that, in addition to his public lectures, the professor gladly gives private seminars on the very same theme to young and not-so-young representatives of the fairer sex, to whom he is happy to introduce the subject; but such things do not concern us right now.

Partly because the subject of today's lecture is not pleasure.

"Let us start from here," Professore Mantegazza says, and, with a sure hand, he draws an uninterrupted horseshoe-shaped line in chalk on the blackboard. "From this parabola, with which we will follow the evolution of our system throughout its course."

If there were a female teacher of mathematics in the hall, she might perhaps object that what Mantegazza has drawn is not a parabola at all, and indeed, when examined closely, is not even a function; but there are no female teachers of mathematics here. There are instead, as we have said, many ladies of all ages: from the young lady in search of a husband, accompanied by her dignified mother, proud to show that her daughter is interested in the latest scientific discoveries; to the noblewoman, complete with puppy and crinoline, who hopes to find in the pleasure of intellectual pursuit what her delicate health, combined with a toad-like appearance, has prevented her from finding in the joys of married life.

And there are, in the majority, men. Men of every kind.

Elegant students in white shirts and waistcoats, smelling of cigars and cologne, and less elegant students, wearing overcoats that would not have been in fashion even when their elder brothers wore them ten years earlier, but never thinking of taking them off because what is underneath is even worse. Gentlemen of a certain age, perhaps merchants, perhaps actors. Perhaps even teachers – but not of mathematics. And, in the last row, a curious fellow.

Curious because, although he is at the back of the hall, he was among those who arrived first: three quarters of an hour ago, to be precise, a time which he has spent reading a small book with an English title. Curious because, given that we have been talking about fashion, this fellow is dressed in top hat and tails, an outfit that would have seemed quite old-fashioned several decades ago; but the garment is made from cloth of an excellent quality, English like the small book and the tailor who probably cut the cloth, and the top hat which he holds propped on his lap is shiny, not because it is worn but because it is new.

In the meantime, Professore Mantegazza has finished writing above the horseshoe a sequence of words, in a beautiful hand: Childhood – Adolescence – Youth – MATURITY – Old Age – Decrepitude.

The man in the top hat smiles beneath whiskers resembling those of a lieutenant in the Austro-Hungarian army and slowly moves his head up and down.

The subject of today's lecture is "life".

A subject about which he knows a fair amount.

Even more, perhaps, than Professore Paolo Mantegazza.

~~~

"Having reached this point," said the professor, "there is one last thing to remember, something which should also be the first in our consciousness."

And, turning to the auditorium, he looked at those present with a satisfied expression.

Nobody had left the hall.

Nobody had abandoned his or her place during the forty-five minutes of the lecture. They were all still there.

The students were there, although this was hardly surprising: leaving during a public lecture by one of your professors, having perhaps sat in the front row, would have been an egregious mistake.

The ladies of various ages were there; Mantegazza knew he could count on the ladies, especially the oldest among them, and the presence of adolescent girls and young wives always put him in a good mood. Their attention satisfied him perhaps even more than their admiration.

His colleagues were there: they often came to his lectures, sometimes to learn, sometimes to envy, sometimes both. He did the same for them, and for the same purposes.

And above all, one of his dearest friends was there, a man Mantegazza had spotted immediately at the beginning of the lecture, even though he was sitting at the back of the hall; one of those discreet presences that Paolo Mantegazza always looked for, and whose presence reassured him considerably when he had to speak in public. A face he knew, with a confident, reliable expression, a face to which he could look for approval, doubt, curiosity, so as to adjust his speech accordingly.

They were all there. Nobody was missing.

"Practising science means above all having foresight, and in the evolution of this ideal line rests the fallibility of our science," Professore Mantegazza said, satisfied but solemn, turning to the parabola behind him and pointing to its right extremity. "That is because we are unable to foresee how much it will bend and curve in the course of our existence. We know that the life of each of us will come to an end, but we are not given to know either how or when."

And finally, you are there, dear reader, of whatever sex, who, in comparison with Professore Paolo Mantegazza and all those attending the lecture, have an unfair advantage. That is, since what you are reading is a mystery story, you are perfectly well aware that within a few pages one of the people you are about to meet will kick the bucket. And, although still ignorant of the precise circumstances of that event, you know perfectly well that he or she will be murdered. Only, you don't know who is about to leave us, or who is responsible.

If you're prepared to be patient, we will get there.

Minus 5

"Well, well, my dear fellow, I see you're in splendid form."

Paolo Mantegazza took the hand held out to him and shook it, sealing the handshake with his left hand placed over the two joined right hands, a gesture halfway between the paternal and the papal.

"I'm content, Professore, I'm content," Pellegrino Artusi replied, regaining possession of his right hand. Mantegazza was a great man, a great physiologist, but when he shook your hand it was as if he were trying to send you to the orthopaedist. Perhaps, obsessed as he was with physical efficiency, he was afraid that other people might have assumed he was on his last legs if he didn't try to break a few of your metacarpals when he shook your hand.

"Nothing to do with contentment," Mantegazza said as he was handed his coat and stick by his assistant. "Take it from a clinician, my dear Pellegrino. Bright eyes, straight back."

And very full belly, Mantegazza thought to himself. Not like me, of course.

Although on the verge of seventy, Mantegazza was well preserved to an enviable degree. The straight, robust, but thin figure, the long flowing hair that had with time turned white but not pink, and finally the military goatee, of the same colour as the mane of hair: in his appearance, Mantegazza recalled General Custer at the age of seventy – if said general had actually reached that age instead of being riddled with bullets at Little Big Horn, of course.

"I thank you, but I do actually think that the secret lies in being content. Talking of being content, I know that it is a small thing compared with all your works, but it would please me to make you a gift of this."

And having taken his left hand from behind his back, Artusi held out to the professor a volume considerably thicker than the one he had been reading before the beginning of the lecture. *Science in the Kitchen and the Art of Eating Well – 1900.*

"Oh, what a beauty. Is it a new edition?"

"Yes, it is. The fifth."

"Oh, very good, my friend, now you only need another ninety-five and you will get what you deserve."

Artusi smiled, a slight blush spreading across his cheeks.

Nine years had passed since Paolo Mantegazza, an unquestioned authority in the field of medicine and health, had devoted two of his lectures to Artusi's cookery manual, thus contributing in no small measure to the wider diffusion of a book that had had no success at first. Meeting Artusi in person for the first time, he had even said to him solemnly:

"You have done a grand job with this book, and I wish you a hundred editions."

It could certainly not be said that Professore Paolo Mantegazza brought bad luck. The first edition of nine years previously (1,000 copies) had soon been followed by a second (again 1,000 copies) and then a third (this time 2,000) followed by a fourth (3,000) and a fifth, the first copy of which Mantegazza was now holding in his hand.

"It seems somewhat more voluminous than the original, or am I mistaken?" the professor said, leafing through the book with his gloved hand.

Artusi nodded gravely. "I've added several new recipes and a small *vade mecum* on hygiene, which I should have particular pleasure in submitting to your attention."

Mantegazza looked at the book he had in his hand and then at Artusi, visibly satisfied at having such trust placed in him; then, having put his coat over his forearm, he took his stick and pointed the silver pommel in the direction of the exit.

"In that case, I shall read it with great pleasure, Signor Artusi. In fact, I'll go further: to make my walk even more pleasant, would you like to accompany me as far as Santa Maria del Fiore? If you have nothing else to do . . ."

Artusi's whiskers tipped upwards, in an invisible but agreeable smile. "On the contrary. I'd be honoured."

☙

"So it seems your work is having considerable success," Mantegazza said, carrying his coat. Even though it was the beginning of October, the heat had not yet made up its mind to leave Florence or the places with which Artusi was familiar. "Five editions, and always with new recipes. How many are there this time?"

"Thirty-five, if I'm not mistaken. Compared with the previous one. Compared with the first edition, there are more than a hundred."

"More than a hundred," said Mantegazza, nodding slowly. "Remarkable. I assume that now, when you go to restaurants or grand hotels, you only have to say your name and the cooks bow down before you."

"Quite the contrary, my dear professor, quite the contrary," Artusi replied. "I don't enjoy a great deal of popularity in the world of professional cooks. I think there's more than one who has wished I would die of cholera. Nobody is more reluctant to yield his secrets – those that make him a great *chef de cuisine* – to a commonplace yokel who wants to make them public, and moreover to make money from them instead of him. No, most people write to me."

"Write to you?"

"Yes, they write to me. Sometimes to correct me, sometimes to tell me the recipe as I've published it isn't the one from their region, sometimes to say, 'If you liked this *dolce di tedescheria*, you should try this other one,' and so on. In short, my book has grown the way a child grows: by listening and learning from other people's experience."

Which was exactly what had happened.

Science in the Kitchen, in its first edition, consisted of 475 recipes; the second, about a hundred more – 104, to be precise. But it was not easy to be pernickety, because letters constantly arrived at Artusi's house on Piazza d'Azeglio: letters ordering the book, which could only be acquired directly from the author, but also, and above all, letters containing new recipes. Recipes that Artusi would read, try, and finally approve, publishing them in the next edition of the book: in short, though he produced in an analogue medium, he was the first blogger of the modern era.

"The way a child grows," Mantegazza repeated: he had a habit of repeating the words spoken by whomever he was talking to, as if thinking that they became clearer when uttered by him, or perhaps it was simply because he was growing ever so slightly senile and wanted to make sure that he had understood correctly. "Unlike us, who are gradually getting older."

"If you are old, Professore Mantegazza, then you should know that I am more than a decade older. If I were to believe that curve of yours, I ought to be decrepit."

"So you disagree with my curve?" said Mantegazza, somewhat surprised perhaps, like all doctors, that common mortals might also have opinions about health and well-being.

"Not at all. It depends what we put on the curve. If we put

a man's abilities, there is no doubt that the trajectory is as you've drawn it. But if we put satisfaction, well, then I must say I disagree. The fact is, my dear professor, in me the joy of living increases with every year that passes."

And this was the second truth of the evening.

The aim of human life is the nutrition and reproduction of the species, as Artusi, a true son of Emilia-Romagna, had written at the beginning of his book; and his youth had indeed been a steady oscillation between these two instincts.

But once past his fifties, which at that time was more a privilege than an age, the hormones of reproduction had given way to the enzymes of digestion, and Artusi had embarked on a more placid life, one that was definitely less unpredictable but equally definitely more satisfactory, thanks to the other privilege which Artusi enjoyed: that of being sure that he would have lunch at midday and dinner at seven, and always at a well-laden table.

Mantegazza nodded. "I understand. You're satisfied with how you live, and I assure you I believe you. On the other hand, you do not seem to ever be satisfied with your book, given that you're constantly changing it."

"Well, I wouldn't say it was dissatisfaction, but rather a blessing. I never tire of adding new dishes, I must admit."

"Then you won't mind if I introduce you to someone. I have a good friend who owns a farm and a small food factory near Val d'Orcia, and who's a great admirer of yours. Just recently he was telling me that it would give him great pleasure to meet you and have you taste some of his raw materials."

So that was it. Another pain in the arse to deal with. Every month since he had publicised the Burchi bakery in Pisa in his book, praising its *schiacciata*, products of every kind arrived in Piazza d'Azeglio, from raw materials to ready-cooked dishes, with a request to taste them. Sometimes – though rarely – good things arrived, more often ordinary things, and quite frequently inedible mush. Almost all of them were accompanied by a letter from the current supplicant, who frequently would have benefitted from lessons in grammar as much as in cooking. But how could he refuse Mantegazza, with all he had done for him?

"It would be an enormous pleasure for me, too. In fact, Professore, if I may take the liberty, it would be a great honour if the two of you would agree to be my guests at dinner this coming Saturday. Obviously, accompanied by your wives."

Mantegazza allowed himself a smile, looking his friend in the whiskers. "Signor Artusi, how could one ever refuse a dinner invitation from you?"

Minus 4

"Excellent, Signor Artusi, absolutely excellent."

"I'm pleased, Signor Gazzolo, I truly am."

Which was true. Inviting a person to dinner, as the great Brillat-Savarin said, means caring about his happiness, and this was a mission that Artusi took very seriously. Even when, as that evening, he had barely met his guest; in fact, more so in such cases. Every amateur cook enjoys being able to entertain a new acquaintance not just with his words, but also with his dishes.

"How do you select a menu to serve your guests?"

"Before anything else, it is necessary to know the guest."

In this case, the choice was quite easy. One of the guests was Professore Mantegazza, who in his immortal *In Praise of Old Age* proclaimed: "An excellent dinner for an elderly person consists of a little cold meat and a good lettuce salad"; all this, be it noted, if the elderly person was someone else. If, on the other hand, his name was Paolo Mantegazza – as Artusi had noted down a little earlier in his diary – then dinner consisted of a first course, two or three main courses, a dessert, three quarter-bottles of wine, and sometimes a little Barolo as a digestive. No hors d'oeuvre, for heaven's sake – that would only make things too heavy.

"And what if you don't know your guest, as is the case this evening?' asked Gazzolo, smiling and tilting his head a little.

Secondo Gazzolo was a big man with small eyes, large hands, a very thick beard which gave the merest glimpse of florid cheeks, and very white teeth. Teeth that were certainly not his, and about whose provenance – ivory, porcelain, an English soldier who had died at Waterloo – Artusi could only speculate. But, if the set of teeth that he flaunted was not his own, many other things were, for one of the few things that Artusi had grasped during the brief time of a dinner was that Secondo Gazzolo was a rich man.

That much was clear from his coat – Casentino cloth of the finest quality – his thick leather shoes and the ring his wife wore on her finger: a genuine diamond set in a crown of yellow gold. An object of old-fashioned design but outstanding value. Gazzolo was a rich man and had been so for some time.

"Well, in that case I have to rely on our mutual acquaintances. You're a friend of Professore Mantegazza's, which presumably means you're a man of pleasant company and lordly tastes."

And so the menu had been that used for only very special guests. As first course, risotto *alla milanese*, as per Recipe no. 80; as a fried course, sole with squid and mushrooms; as a stew, fricassee of milk heifer, as in no. 256; and as a roast, a nice leg of wether (no. 530). Then they had moved on to dessert, or rather, desserts: for the gentlemen, cake with pine nuts (no. 582), and for the ladies, a *biscotto* served with *zabaglione* according to the dictates of no. 683. After which the ladies had got out of the way and left the men in the sitting room, ready to talk about business.

"Yes, indeed, the professor and I have known each other for some time," Gazzolo confirmed.

"Since 1880, if I'm not mistaken. That's how far back our friendship goes."

Mantegazza threw his friend a look of deep affection, such as only a litre of wine in the body can cause.

This was the second thing that Artusi had grasped about Secondo Gazzolo. That he was a pleasant man, and that he had many friends.

Partly because having him as an enemy was probably not advisable.

"However you did it, you hit the mark. I love fricassee, and fried mushrooms, too. But I must confess that serving them in that way, with fried squid, I didn't know. It isn't in your book, is it?"

"Not explicitly, no."

"I was sure of it. I know your book inside out, were you aware of that? You should include it as a recipe. It's hard to fry squid in such a way that it still tastes like squid. Usually, one feels as if one is eating one of those rubber tyres they put on automobiles these days."

"That's because people take medium-sized squid and cut them into pieces," Artusi said, calmly and authoritatively. "If you want to make a fried dish out of squid, you have to use those very small ones, the kind they call *calamaretti* in Naples. Or else you need to cut the squid into rings, not pieces. Thin rings. That way you obtain a nice ring of fried breading, and the squid in the middle is just for support, or almost. The taste and texture come from the breading."

"That's true. Everything's better fried, even cholera, as my mother used to say."

"Was it your mother who taught you all these things about cookery?"

"No, not at all. Or perhaps, yes, who knows? I was little. As the professor will have told you, I have a farm in the Sienese hills, from where I come."

"And you should see what a farm," Mantegazza said. "Large, but that's not all. Equipped with every technological discovery in support of hygiene and productivity. Electric light. Motor-driven agricultural equipment. And now also food preservation."

"Food preservation?"

"Precisely. I've started a small canning factory on the premises."

"Ah, I see. Like Signor Cirio's canned tomatoes."

"With all due respect to the Cirio company, who were pioneers, we are much more advanced."

"You should see Signor Gazzolo's factory," said Mantegazza. "It's truly in the vanguard. It has vacuum sealing, it has appertisation, it even has a dry ice machine."

"And what is that for?"

"I'm setting up an ice-cream-making plant to use the leftover milk. It's more profitable than a cheese factory. The dry ice is for taking the ice cream home: it keeps it cold and stops it getting wet, but it can also be used for meat. Actually, the thing I'm proudest of is the vacuum sealing for preserved meats. We don't stop at appertisation, we go further than that."

"Apper . . . ?"

"The process of sterilising canned food by cooking it at high temperatures," Mantegazza translated, proud to insert a little science into the conversation after all that cookery. "The food is exposed to temperatures over a hundred degrees for between thirty minutes and an hour. In that way, the bacteria, toxins and fungi that fester in the food are killed."

"And the meat turns as hard as iron and disgusting to eat," Gazzolo went on, less scientifically but more conscientiously. "It's a process suitable for vegetables that have an acid component, for fish that is in itself tender and not fibrous, but meat – oh, no! Meat should be cooked slowly, and at low temperatures. I produce canned meat that has been cooked already seasoned, at low temperatures, and is then preserved through vacuum sealing."

"And how do you do this vacuum sealing?"

"With machinery patented by an American inventor named Edison."

By now, if they had not been talking about things to eat, Artusi would probably have been lost in contemplation of the wonderfully modular nature of science. Every new scientific discovery, if it is a genuine one, goes far beyond the solving of the problem for which it was devised. Like a single piece of Lego, we can use it to build whatever we like, even the words *Lego doesn't work* made up of pieces of Lego.

In the same way, the very principle that allowed Thomas Alva Edison to extract air from glass bulbs, for the purpose of manufacturing efficient lights, could be used to extract air from a steel pot, for the purpose of making ragù. However, since they were talking about food, Pellegrino's interest was focused on more practical aspects. And being, basically, a businessman, the first practical aspect that came into his mind was almost an obvious one.

"It's going to cost you a fortune. How much do you sell your canned meat for?"

"Don't believe it, Signor Artusi. In fact, the vacuum-sealing process makes it possible to cook at lower temperatures and for less time, with a considerable saving in energy. This in turn makes it possible to lower the costs of production. In addition, the vacuum sealing is carried out at the canning phase. The meat is placed in the can with the flavouring and vacuum sealed before it's cooked. That allows for notably longer preservation times. And it also makes it easier to sell."

"The food of the future, my dear Artusi, the food of the future," the Barolo said in an authoritative tone through Professore Mantegazza's mouth.

"That may well be so, I suppose. I'd be curious to taste it. Can it easily be found in delicatessens?"

"Alas, at the moment it is not on sale."

"When do you plan to put it on the market?"

"That has yet to be decided. But I plan to do so as soon as possible, and with that in mind, the opinion of the most reputable gastronome in the Kingdom would be of great help to us.'

Artusi smiled like someone modestly accepting a compliment.

"The fact is, we've only recently started production. What's more, we've just had a very large order from a customer who can't be ignored, and for a while our output will be devoted entirely to them. But if you want to taste my product, I would be more than happy to send you a few samples as a gift."

Artusi bowed his head briefly, as if to say that he thanked his guest for the kind gift, but that for the moment such a thing was not at the forefront of his thoughts.

"A customer who can't be ignored," Mantegazza remarked, drumming his fingers on the table. "He must have a very large number of mouths to feed."

Artusi looked at Gazzolo, evidently thinking exactly the same thing.

Gazzolo smiled like someone who's got there before anyone else. "Absolutely, Professore Mantegazza. An army, no less. A great army, guarding a great gate, a Sublime Porte."

Eyebrows raised, Pellegrino Artusi looked from Gazzolo to Mantegazza, then back to Gazzolo.

"Just so," Gazzolo went on, showing his false teeth in a genuine, self-satisfied smile. "I'm speaking about the army of the Ottoman Empire."

"And how on earth did you manage to enter into trade with the Ottoman Empire?"

"Oh, that's a long story. Just imagine, it dates back to 1875."

"The year I moved to this house," Artusi replied, with an inviting smile. And I'm not moving from it until you tell me the story, the smile said.

~☙~

It was important to know, Gazzolo began, that up until 1875 the Ottoman Empire had only survived thanks to loans from the great European banks. The Crimean War had depleted the coffers of the Sultan, who even twenty years earlier had already started asking London for credit. For the record, the Sultan's name was Abdul Mejid, but that didn't really matter, because he'd died in 1861 and the one who came after him had continued to behave in the same way, borrowing money and not paying it back.

"Now, the Ottoman administration was not familiar with the European credit system," Gazzolo continued. "We're used to paying bills within thirty days, debts within a year, loans within ten years. But not there. Oh, no. There, it was cash on the barrel. You paid straight away. And if you didn't, they cut off your hands and so on."

The ease of obtaining money on loan, without the risk of losing your hands, had gone to the heads of the Ottoman administrators; rather as happens now with people who take out a loan to buy an SUV, then get another loan to pay off the first one, and then one day someone comes to their house and takes everything away, even the floor. That was why the Ottomans had continued to pile up debts until 1875, when the Empire defaulted, as we would say today, or, as they said then, declared bankruptcy. In short, just to be clear, it went bust. And when you go bust, you're at the mercy of your creditors.

If you're a car mechanic, you end up in the hands of a bank; if you're an empire, you end up in the hands of another empire. But the Sublime Porte was too vast an empire to be absorbed or annexed by a single European power. What ensued at that point was a carve-up.

This carve-up took the form, at first, of the creation of the OPDA, the Ottoman Public Debt Administration, which ...

Renegotiated the debt and helped the Ottomans to overcome the crisis? you might be thinking to yourself.

How wrong you are. No, what it actually did was provide further guarantees that allowed the Ottomans to contract further debts. Debts that were used to allow European companies to build infrastructure on their territory, in such a way that, as the Italian ambassador in Constantinople wrote to Prime Minister Crispi in 1890: "The Turks will be completely in our power when all their usable resources have been mortgaged."

In other words, and to put it in technical terms, by the end of the nineteenth century Europe had the Sublime Porte by the balls.

⁓ᴥ⁓

"Forgive me, Signor Gazzolo, but I don't follow you," said Artusi, in a polite tone. "I knew that these loans had been contracted with the great London banks and the Austro-Hungarian insurance companies. But where does Italy come into all this?"

"She comes into it quite a lot. You see, Signor Artusi, the governing council of the OPDA has always had an Italian as its head. The first was Avvocato Francesco Mancardi, followed for three years, up until '93, by Signor Simondetti. The council is currently presided over by Everardo D'Ancona."

Gazzolo took a cigar of disturbing dimensions from his waistcoat, cut off the tip with a little pocketknife and lit it with evident satisfaction.

"The aim of the OPDA has changed over time. At first, it managed and collected the finances of the Ottoman state. The Ottomans had granted their creditors, that is, the European banks, a monopoly on salt, silk and tobacco. In practice, the taxes on these goods were collected not by the Ottomans, but by the banks."

"Salt, silk and tobacco," said Mantegazza.

"Precisely. Except for cigars, I don't know why."

Gazzolo took a particularly inspired drag of his own, clearly thinking that if it had been up to him, he would have obtained a monopoly even on underpants. "But now, as I was telling you, things have changed. In practice, the Ottomans, in order to set up great construction projects, like bridges, railways, advanced technology, have to turn to Europe. Signor D'Ancona has two tasks at present: on the one hand, to make sure that the Turkish buyers are reliable. To evaluate their solvency. In short, to work out which ones will actually pay. On the other, to evaluate the credibility and quality of the European products to be offered in exchange. To estimate the credentials of the companies concerned. In short, to establish that there's no cheating likely from either party."

Gazzolo was silent for a moment, just long enough to puff at his cigar.

"And such an appointment is governmental, I imagine," said Artusi.

Smiling and blowing out smoke, Gazzolo shook his head. "For all the other countries, yes. The delegates of Great Britain, France, Germany and the Austro-Hungarians are all manipulated by their governments. D'Ancona is appointed by the Chamber of Commerce and works on its behalf. Even against the political interests of foreign governments, if necessary."

Gazzolo slowly exhaled a vast cloud of smoke, which Artusi took, not as a sign of storms ahead, but as a good omen.

Being a good businessman, Artusi had his own inner governing council, consisting of Pellegrino Artusi, Artusi Pellegrino and the owner of the house at 10 Piazza D'Azeglio. And the role of this council, too, had changed over time. At first, it had mainly been concerned with non-repayable investments; then, with the advancing of age, it had specialised in the accumulation of reserve funds. In short, as happens to most of us, the prodigal young Artusi had been replaced by an older, wiser, and above all stingier Artusi. Our good friend Pellegrino had always liked money and had always been of the firm opinion that you could never have enough of it.

"What you're basically telling me is that we Italians are particularly favoured to do business with the Ottoman government, because we're more independent?"

"In the final analysis, that is indeed so."

"In that case, my dear Gazzolo, I have a favour to ask of you."

"Let me guess," said Gazzolo, smiling through the cigar smoke like a big friendly dragon. "You used to trade in textiles, am I correct?"

"Actually, I'd say I've never stopped. English textiles, silk, brocades from the Orient. They're very much coming back into fashion now."

"Well, in that case, perhaps you would like to meet Signor D'Ancona in person. He will be my guest in two weeks' time, together with various other industrialists and entrepreneurs from Central Italy. If you don't have any other engagements for the end of that week . . ."

"No engagements, I assure you, Signor Gazzolo."

From the diary of Pellegrino Artusi

Florence, 15 October, 1900

Today I received in my house on Piazza d'Azeglio, by parcel post, a few samples of the canned meat of which we spoke at dinner some days ago. They were accompanied by a letter from Signor Gazzolo, who thanked me for my willingness, asked me to give him my judgement in a blunt and honest manner and ended with a paean to packaged food. Gazzolo maintains, in agreement with Professore Mantegazza, that this will be the food of the future: well, if such is the case, I am glad that I am old. I much prefer the purgatory that surely awaits me over the hell of having to eat such awful stuff.

❧

One day, perhaps, someone will invent a suitable tool for opening cans of industrial food; until that day, each of us will have to manage with his own means, as Francesco and I set out to do today, he holding the accursed can tight with his arms stretched out on the table, to avoid anything spurting on his face and body, while I attempted to force the lid with a large nail. It may be the vacuum-sealing process, or it may be the quality of the tin used, the fact remains that the object proved recalcitrant to all our efforts, which, according to Marietta, looked more like a clumsy attempt to crucify one another to the table than the preparation of something to eat. However, after a considerable length of time, and only thanks to a more powerful blow, the confounded thing yielded, and we were able to liberate its contents.

~⚜~

If opening it was an ordeal, eating it was even worse. The meat, although not hard, was ferrous and fibrous, like beef that was too old, but this sanguineous sensation lasted only a moment before being dominated by the seasoning in the sauce, which was spicy beyond all imagining.

I am not accustomed to chilli pepper and its cathartic powers, and I immediately felt the effects. In the course of the meal, I was forced several times to have recourse to the carafe of water; after dinner, though, I was forced to have recourse, not to the carafe, but to the toilet bowl. The truth is that I had a new convenience installed only a few days ago, but I certainly had not imagined such a solemn inauguration: long processions between the bedroom and the comfort station, complete with heartfelt invocations to the Almighty, thanks to which I may have gained myself further decades in purgatory. And now here I am, with a steaming bowl of camomile, trying to console my poor, devastated stomach for the results of this culinary experiment of mine.

~⚜~

In his letter, Gazzolo confirmed to me that next week he will be visited by the intermediary for trade with the Ottomans, Signor D'Ancona, that they will be joined by a number of other entrepreneurs to spend what the English call a weekend, and that my company would be much appreciated. There will be an

opportunity, I sincerely hope, to discuss future business. Tomor-
row morning, therefore, I shall write to Gazzolo and gratefully
accept his invitation, but as for my publicising of his diabolical
concoction, I fear he will just have to do without it.

Minus 3

Should you wish to visit the manor farm of the castle of Campoventoso, the first thing to do is wrap up warm.

If you go in winter, you seriously risk becoming ill: the farm comprises a central body (the castle) which is about one kilometre from the canning factory, which in its turn is separated from the cowsheds by a magnificent field of about nine hectares, square in shape, which means that to cross it you would have to trudge for about three hundred metres across a plain in one of the windiest valleys in Italy; the commonest wind in these parts is the *tramontana*, which means that, since the cowsheds are to the south, you would have the wind behind you.

Should you wish to reach the pigsties, you would have to walk another hundred metres or so, still with the wind behind you. To then return to the castle would be another 1,400 metres, but this time against the wind.

If you go in summer, the wind is less of a problem, but even if there were any wind you would not notice it, because you would be surrounded by clouds of mosquitoes and horseflies, which would probably absorb all your attention. In this case, too, wrapping yourself up is advised.

If on the other hand you go in autumn, there is still wind, but it's less cold, because it usually rains, and rain, as we know, lowers the temperature. So no umbrellas: you would lose them even more easily than usual. Better to wear a good raincoat, and above all a pair of boots.

They will be necessary.

"I wonder if it was really necessary," said Signor Viterbo, looking down at his black calfskin shoes, now irredeemably veined with every shade of mud.

Artusi, who was beside him, did not reply. At least not immediately. He, too, was contemplating his footwear, which at the beginning of the walk had perfectly matched his suit (in other words, black) and now perfectly matched the autumn landscape (in other words, brown).

"I suppose our host is particularly proud of his estate," Artusi remarked, lifting his gaze from his shoes and looking into the distance, where Secondo Gazzolo could be seen conversing in an amiable manner with one of the other guests.

The weekend at the castle of Campoventoso had begun, as was the practice, with a tour of the castle and the estate in order to orientate the new guest, Signor Pellegrino Artusi from Forlimpopoli, who had been duly impressed with the castle and what was inside it.

At the beginning of the tour, the party had been received in the west drawing room, a huge, tastefully decorated room watched over from above by a majestic Bohemian chandelier in Art Nouveau style: a wonderful object, which matched to perfection the breadth and elegance of the room and everything it contained, with the exception of the two bishops. These were two horrible wooden polychrome statues from the Val Gardena, standing on either side of the fireplace, that depicted – so another guest had deigned to inform him – Saint Carlo Borromeo and Saint François de Sales, pillars of the counter-reformation. Obviously, this guest knew all about them and appreciated them, unlike Artusi, who, as a native of Emilia-Romagna, was anticlerical and had good taste.

"With good reason," Signor Viterbo replied. "It's a fine, large estate – 1,200 hectares, partly arable and partly used for raising cattle, including top prize winners at fairs throughout the nation. It's the most valuable agricultural property in the whole province."

"Is that so?"

Signor Viterbo looked around for a moment, giving up, as had Artusi, on contemplating the disaster on his feet. "I know it for a fact. I handled the sale, back when Signor Gazzolo acquired it from Conte Pepoli. And I valued it recently, for Signor D'Ancona as it happens. I'm very familiar with it."

Pellegrino Artusi nodded slowly.

He himself had long been familiar, even if only by name, with Signor Corrado Viterbo, director of the Banca Commerciale Italiana (Florence branch), who had the reputation of being an intelligent, cautious man of great integrity. Surrounding his name there were only good reports; surrounding his person, on the other hand, there was a suit of exquisite cut and exorbitant size, which wrapped and contained one of the fattest men Artusi had ever seen – while Viterbo had been looking at his shoes earlier, Artusi had caught himself wondering if he was able to lace them up by himself.

"So, you're here for the purpose of evaluating the state of health of the businesses that are hoping to be awarded contracts?"

"Precisely. My role is to guarantee that such businesses are in good shape from a financial and productive point of view. As far as Signor Gazzolo's company is concerned, as you will see, there are no problems on that front. My counterpart on the other side is Signor Aliyan. In other words, the person who is speaking with your friend."

Viterbo moved his eyes to the right – one of the few movements he was able to perform quickly – and Artusi followed the direction of his gaze until it reached the slender figure of Professore Paolo Mantegazza, walking beside a man who gesticulated as he spoke.

"Is the gentleman Turkish?" he asked.

~~~

"Of course he's Turkish," said Bartolomeo, superciliously. "He's the Ottoman delegate to the OPDA. Or do you think the Ottomans are so improvident as to trust themselves completely to foreigners?"

"No, no, of course not," Crocetta replied, closing a large suitcase. "I just thought Turks were a bit different."

The maid's surprise was not completely misplaced. Most Italians, especially at the end of the nineteenth century, imagined Turks to be short, dark men who were born with moustaches and caftans. The man who had entrusted the suitcase to her, on the other hand, was one metre ninety tall, as straight as a rod, with fair hair and – had she had time to notice them when he introduced himself to her in perfect Italian – eyes as green as a field of clover.

"And I thought you'd already finished with Signor Aliyan's luggage. May I remind you that the rooms need to be ready before the gentlemen return from their tour of the estate, and right now Signor Aliyan's room and Signor D'Ancona's room haven't been done yet."

Crocetta raised her eyes to heaven, taking advantage of the fact that she had her back to Bartolomeo and he couldn't see her.

From the day she was born, the life of Crocifissa Maggio had been characterised by one expectation: that she obey. Everybody.

Her mother, who had given her that horrible name against which she tried to rebel ("Call me Crocetta, at least that way people don't cross themselves when I appear"). Signor Gazzolo, whom Bartolomeo called "the master". And Bartolomeo himself, who wasn't bad, but was the kind of person who was only content when someone told him what to do.

"Don't worry, Signor Bartolomeo. I'll do Signor D'Ancona's room as soon as I've finished putting away the Turk's things. That's as long as they don't keep changing rooms just as they please . . ."

Bartolomeo coughed. "Signor Aliyan, as we domestics should insist on calling him, gave up his room to Signor D'Ancona because of his state of health, and kindly consented to move to another room."

Kindly my arse, Crocetta thought, although she didn't say it. Firstly because if she'd uttered a bad word in Bartolomeo's presence within the sacred walls of the castle, he would have fainted. And secondly, because he would have had her dismissed. Anyway, "kindly" definitely wasn't accurate. The Turk had kicked up all kinds of fuss, and they hadn't heard the last of it.

While Crocetta was putting the finishing touches to the room, still with her back to her superior, Bartolomeo sighed heavily. There was no way she could know this, but Bartolomeo was thinking more or less the same thing.

Bartolomeo Cattoni had been the butler to the Gazzolo household since before the castle had been home to the Gazzolo household, when it had been the residence of Conte Cornelio Pepoli, direct descendant of that Sicinio Pepoli who had been a correspondent and friend of the legendary singer Carlo Broschi, known as Farinelli, the greatest castrato of the eighteenth century; and, from a professional point of view, Bartolomeo felt more or less like the great Farinelli – metaphorically speaking, of course.

Having passed from Conte Pepoli to a mere grain merchant

had struck him at first as insufferable; but it would have been even more insufferable to abandon the house where he had grown up. Where he had taken his first steps as a groom, had as a young man become valet to Conte Cornelio and had finally been promoted to butler after his predecessor, Signor Costanzo Corrado, had been mistaken for a boar and shot dead by the count himself, way back in November 1886.

Then, one fine day, Conte Cornelio, who had a talent for any activity that involved squandering money, had acted like the Ottoman Empire – on a small scale, but enough to oblige him to sell what had not already been sold or mortgaged, including the estate in Tuscany and the castle, which had been acquired by Secondo Gazzolo with all the staff thrown in. In any case, by that point the count would not have been in a position to maintain even a goldfish.

Then Signor Gazzolo had taken a mediaeval ruin and transformed it into a business, a place of progress; and while, on the one hand, this had increased the prestige of the owner and therefore of the estate, on the other hand it had diminished that of the butler, who had seen himself demoted until he became less important than the estate manager. But the master was the master, and above all the castle was the castle.

And so Bartolomeo had remained at the castle, serving sherry or Barolo Chinato to guests of a rank noticeably inferior to that of the count. Some, although lacking in airs and graces, were acceptable, others, like Signor Reza Kemal Aliyan, decidedly insufferable.

Signor Gazzolo had had the warmest room in the house reserved for Signor Reza Kemal Aliyan, a room to the south, where the *tramontana* was less insistent and where there was a fine large fireplace; but Signor Reza Kemal Aliyan had insisted on giving up his room to Signor D'Ancona, who had a troublesome cold. After which, finding a suitable replacement room for him had been quite an undertaking.

Typical of Levantines: excessively polite and punctilious, always bowing and scraping, and then when it comes down to it, they always find a way to give you a hard time. In that, yes, he was definitely Turkish, though God knows from where. Turkey is a large country.

"But what was it he didn't like, if you don't mind my asking, Signor Bartolomeo?"

꙳

"There wasn't any light. It was the right size, but there was no light. And there was a fireplace. I don't need a fire, never used one." With a peremptory gesture, like someone who thinks using a fire is immoral, Signor Aliyan moved something imaginary away from himself. "I'm from Kars, which is in the north of Anatolia, in the mountains. Don't go thinking I suffer from the cold, just because I'm a Turk."

Mantegazza nodded pensively.

As a traveller who had visited the four corners of the earth, who had ventured into the forests of the Amazon and the islands of the Indies, he knew that not all peoples are as you expect them to be. For that reason, he was not unduly surprised to see a fair-haired, green-eyed Turk.

What surprised him more was how much this fellow talked. And how much he gesticulated. It was as if he were conducting an orchestra.

"Anyway, I said to him: 'I'm infinitely grateful, my dear Signor Gazzolo, for your kindness'" – the Turk's hands came together in a kind of rapid gesture of gratitude, then opened and reached upwards, as if in a symbolic offering not devoid of a certain air of threat – "'but I would infinitely prefer it if you granted this room to D'Ancona *effendi*. D'Ancona *effendi* is older than me'" – the Turk's hand bent, as if imitating an elderly man walking – "'and of more delicate health. I am sure he will appreciate a room with a fire somewhat more than I would. I'" – he concluded for now, pointing his finger at his chest – "'will be absolutely fine in a room that does not have one.'"

Taking a quick breath, Mantegazza ventured: "If you enjoy a good constitution, then sleeping in a room that's not too warm is certainly healthy. Not to mention that the weather is unsettled at the moment."

Freezing cold, Mantegazza would have liked to say, had it not been for the fact that the Turk, appearing not to notice that someone else was trying to speak, continued:

"Then they wanted to give me a room facing west, but I was forced to refuse. I need the sun through the window in the morning." The Turk's hands opened in a gesture similar to that of a referee calling for the VAR. "The light isn't good here, I need light to write and work. 'You work even at weekends?' Signor Gazzolo asked me. 'Of course,' I replied. I think he was impressed."

Mantegazza sighed.

Apart from the fact that Paolo Mantegazza was a university professor, and therefore not accustomed to someone else speaking, it was also the case that the Turk was one of those people who do not know how to respect the rhythm of a conversation. One of those insufferable creatures who do not realise that other people might also have something to say. It would be tiresome even if he were saying interesting things; but, apart from anything else, he was talking about things that did not matter a jot to anybody. His own work, for instance, or his own day, or his own health. Or anything else that involved starting a sentence with the pronoun "I".

"'With you, the deal is done,' I said, 'but D'Ancona *effendi* and I have many other proposals to examine'" – Aliyan counted imaginary papers on his fingers and tapped his left hand on the pocket of his waistcoat, corresponding to the bulge of his watch – "'and very little time in which to do so.'"

~~❧~~

"Yes, of course, I agree. A weekend is too little time to seal a deal. And yet . . ."

Signor Viterbo took a long drag on his cigar, then put his hand behind his back again and continued walking.

"And yet, my dear Signor Artusi, we are not here today to seal a deal. Today we are here to start getting to know one another, to establish in the first place a relationship of mutual respect."

"I very much agree," Artusi replied.

"But in order to establish this relationship, I need to talk to that blasted D'Ancona fellow before anything else. Instead of which, Gazzolo has practically abducted him and is now giving him a guided tour of the estate."

Gazzolo's massive figure could indeed be seen in the distance. He was talking to a man who walked beside him at a slow, diplomatic pace, a tall man with a clean-shaven face and indistinct features – particularly indistinct if you were eighty years old and that man was a hundred metres away.

After another pensive drag on his cigar, Viterbo addressed Artusi without looking at him. "Obviously it's different if the name of the person is already known, and he has already demonstrated a great head for business. Let's say, for instance, a silk merchant who has written and published a book of gastronomy under his own auspices and made a considerable profit out of it."

While Artusi arched his eyebrows (and his whiskers with

them, thanks to the myofascial and cutaneous structure of the face), Viterbo turned to him.

"My dear Signor Artusi, I am here to do business, just as you are. And if Signor D'Ancona had not manifested an interest in you, you wouldn't even have been invited. The current situation is this: we have a contract that we are happily concluding with Signor Gazzolo's company and other potential representatives whose possible inclusion we are verifying."

A pause, a puff on his cigar, smoke spreading rapidly in the direction of the cowsheds, driven by the wind. Followed by silence. Unlike the Turk, Pellegrino Artusi had a very clear idea of the right time to talk and the right time to listen: a discipline learned in many years of trade, and never to be over-estimated.

"Commercial relations with the Sublime Porte are very delicate, Signor Artusi," Viterbo went on. "At the moment the presidency of the governing council of the OPDA is ours, Italy's I mean, but it would only take one false move to make a hash of it all. Please forgive me for saying things that must be obvious to a man of your experience, but with every deal it is necessary to observe the maximum caution."

Artusi smiled good-naturedly. "That is all the better, I assure you, Signor Viterbo. I'm not the kind of man who would expend money and effort on a futile undertaking, I find it quite reassuring to be surrounded by people of the same disposition. It's a strange thing, for a man of my age, to be subject to scrutiny, but I fear I will have to adapt."

"At least you're in good company," Viterbo replied, also smiling.

"Precisely. Do you by any chance know who the others are?"

"The others, or perhaps I should say the other." Viterbo smiled again. "Over there, near the row of cypresses, is Signor Bonci, chief accountant of a major insurance company, the Compagnia Granducale di Sicurtà."

"Ah, Signor Bonci," Artusi said, recognising the man who had informed him of the identity of the saints. "And I assume the young woman with him is his daughter."

"That's correct," Viterbo said, his smile growing more pronounced. "Her name is Delia."

～☆～

"Papa, he's old."

"So are you, my dear Delia. You're nearly twenty-four. It's to be hoped that he likes you, because if he doesn't nobody will ever take you."

"Papa, he's fat."

"I should hope so," said Signor Bonci, looking into the distance, his hands behind his back. "Rich men are fat, Delia."

Strictly speaking, Signor Bonci was not exactly skinny himself; but, if it had only been a question of weight, his appearance would probably have been acceptable. Unfortunately, Signor Bonci was not just ugly, he was truly grotesque: a round little man with an even rounder head, to the bottom of which clung a thick, unruly little beard, and to the top a comb-over glued tenaciously to the skull with some unknown material. Between these two incongruous hirsute appendages was a red face adorned with a vast collection of moles of all kinds, which made Signor Bonci look less like a man and more like a watermelon with a fake beard.

"But he's too fat," Delia retorted, looking at her father, her big eyes wide open in dismay. "He looks as if he's been blown up with a pump."

Signor Bonci looked at his daughter with affection. And with admiration. Because Delia really was beautiful. Everything in her was beautiful: her slightly almond-shaped eyes, her small soft mouth, her upturned little nose. By the beginning of the twentieth century, people had been arguing for years as to whether or not Charles Darwin's theory of evolution was a plausible explanation for man's appearance; well, anyone who had seen Delia Bonci and compared her with her father would have had to conclude, in accordance with Darwin, that not only do human beings evolve and improve, but they sometimes do so in a decidedly spectacular fashion.

"Have you only just noticed that?" Bonci said with a languid smile. "We've been seeing him for months."

"Yes, but you didn't ask me to marry him before."

"Hush now, Delia, my dear. Before anything else, Signor Viterbo must ask *me* for your hand, not you. When, and above all if, he asks for it. Let's not put the cart before the horse. But I have reason to believe that everything will work out well. I've seen how he greeted you, and the consideration with which he asked if you would be accompanying me this weekend. Trust me, my darling. In my opinion, he's in love."

"Yes, but . . ."

"But?"

"I'm not in love with him."

"Give it time, my daughter. Once you're married, you, too, will fall in love with him. That's what happened to your mother and me."

Actually, Mother hated you, Delia would gladly have said to her father if only she'd had the courage. They all hate you. That's why nobody wants me. Not because I'm not beautiful, or because I'm not likely to have a sizeable dowry. They're all terrified at the prospect of having you as a father-in-law. You're intrusive, overbearing, rude, greedy and stingy. If only you knew what I think of you. But you do know, you do know, only you don't give a hoot.

"Trust me, my dear," Bonci had continued in the meantime, still with his hands behind his back. "Papa won't last forever, you know. And Signor Viterbo is a fine man. Above all, he's a man of substance. You will have all you need, my child."

⁓⁂⁓

"Good. Now all we need is Signor D'Ancona, and we'll have finished. It won't take long, but it's better if I give you a hand."

Crocetta nodded, putting the suitcase on the bed and starting to loosen the straps. In fact, this was the fourth time that D'Ancona had stayed with them, and Crocetta was starting to know and fear his luggage. A suitcase, a toiletries bag, a trunk for the clothes, a small, locked briefcase, a shoe bag. While Crocetta removed the shirts from the suitcase, Bartolomeo opened the door.

"You arrange the personal effects in the room, I'll see to the pigeons."

And then, of course, there were the pigeons. The pigeons always came with Signor D'Ancona. There were four of them, two with a pink band on the right foot, and two with a black band. Once released, the former would head for Rome, the latter for Milan.

"But why does Signor D'Ancona still use pigeons? Wouldn't it be quicker to use the telephone?"

"A telephone call can be listened to by anyone, both at this end and at the other end. And Signor D'Ancona's calls are often of a private nature."

"Well, he could write. Now we also have the mail cart, he doesn't need to go to town anymore."

"They are of a private nature and also require a certain speed." Bartolomeo bent down to get the cage with the birds. "A letter would take a couple of days to travel from here to Rome."

It's true: by that time, the mail between large cities functioned with remarkable swiftness. A letter sent from Milan in the morning arrived in Florence during the day, and in cities like Turin there were deliveries within the day – people invited each other to afternoon tea by post. But there were much quicker methods.

"A pigeon, on the other hand, would take a few hours. The ability to communicate news as soon as possible is of vital importance to Signor D'Ancona's work, and the pigeon remains the quickest bearer of messages over such distances."

"That may be so. For me, a pigeon's only worth something when it's well roasted. By the way, do you know what they're having for dinner?"

Crocetta's question was not entirely disinterested. Dinners in the Gazzolo household, which were copious on normal occasions, became positively Babylonian when guests were present. Often more than one portion of the delectable food was left over, and when that happened the staff would feel perfectly free to polish off what their employers had sent back to the kitchen.

"An exotic dish, as far as I know." Bartolomeo, already in the corridor, placed a hand on the doorknob. "In honour of our Ottoman guest. Signora Clara is dealing with it personally."

"An exotic dish? What might that be?"

"I think it's called *cuscussù*," Bartolomeo said as the door closed behind him.

Minus 2

"I had never tasted it before. Did you know it?"

"Oh, yes," said Bonci. "When I was in Tripoli, it was the only thing anyone ate. But they make it quite a lot in Istanbul, too." He turned to his daughter. "In fact, we almost feel at home in Istanbul by now, don't we?"

His daughter nodded, without saying a word, her eyes fixed on her plate.

"And you, signora, who taught it to you?" Viterbo asked, turning his gaze to the hostess.

"Well, everything I've learned about cooking I've learned from that gentleman there," said Signora Clara Gazzolo, smiling in the direction of a man sitting on the other side of the table: Pellegrino Artusi, obviously.

"You do me too much honour, Signora Clara."

The room to the west of the castle, the one most appropriate for hosting a lunch for nine, had welcomed the weekend guests after their morning tour of the estate, supplying them first of all with a refuge, then with a lot of light and, above all, a lot of heat. Both these sources of comfort derived from fire: the heat, from two huge fireplaces on the long sides of the room, and the light from a huge crystal chandelier studded with candles.

As soon as the guests had reached a temperature compatible with sociability and were once more able to move their fingers, the food had arrived: waiters bringing silver trays with measured steps, while Bartolomeo proceeded majestically and confidently around the table, as if the house itself were shifting beneath him as he moved his feet.

"Not at all," Signora Gazzolo replied. "When compliments are deserved, they should be uttered. And besides, I also wanted to put myself to the test. How often do I get the opportunity to have the author of one's favourite cookbook taste one of his own dishes?"

Pellegrino Artusi's politeness was put on the alert. If he had said, "I certainly don't hold it against you," that would have been a little like saying, "There's no way I'm coming back and having dinner here with you, you old crone." If, conversely, he had said something like "But I hope this certainly won't be the last time I taste your dishes," it would have been a little like inviting himself to dinner.

"A particularly felicitous choice," Artusi replied, rising above the question. "May I ask you why you chose that particular dish?"

"So you liked it?" the hostess asked, evidently convinced that compliments, when timely, should always be uttered, especially if addressed to her.

"Executed to perfection," Artusi assured her, having wiped his whiskers with his napkin. "Especially as it is one of the most tiresome and complicated procedures in my little book. The dish is a real bother to make, which is why I repeat my congratulations and thank you for having devoted so much time to making us welcome."

That was probably enough grovelling to the hostess. To tell the truth, her work had ended with the choice of dish; it was the butler who had done the shopping, the cook who had cooked and the waiters who had served. After which the hostess had received congratulations from all the dinner guests. Missing from these guests was Contessa Maria Fantoni, the wife of Professore Paolo Mantegazza, who, although having been invited to accompany her husband, had preferred to remain at home. As is the way with true aristocrats, the invitation had been declined both in writing ("This tiresome autumn sickness that afflicts me would not allow me to fully enjoy your company") and orally ("Who? Gazzolo? You must be mad. I already spent an evening with his vulture of a wife, and I felt like jumping out of the window to escape. Imagine me spending two days in the house of that nouveau-riche old bitch").

"Speaking of making us welcome, I must congratulate you on the choice of candles," said Mantegazza, with the air of a man about town. "I find they create quite a different effect compared with electric light."

Signora Clara laughed. "For heaven's sake, don't tell my husband. As far as he's concerned, anything that isn't electric makes his flesh crawl. But in my opinion, one can't install a genuine Max Ritter von Spaun chandelier and put electric bulbs in it, can one?"

"Of course not," Gazzolo said, with an air of condescending forbearance. "As long as you're prepared to change the candles every week, instead of turning a light switch. Not to mention pulling it down, and putting it back up, and pulling it back down and putting it back up. It weighs just over a ton, and the mechanism cost me even more than the thing itself. Professore Mantegazza, if you encourage my wife that way, I won't invite you anymore, you can be sure of that."

"That would indeed be a pity. Especially after the delicacies you served us this evening."

"So you liked them?" the signora asked.

"Absolutely exquisite," Corrado Viterbo assured her in his lilting Umbrian accent, looking towards the soup tureen, from which he had already been served twice. "All the more so in that, if I may be allowed—"

"No, please, please! No more compliments. Rather, if any-body should want some more . . ."

"If only I could," said Signor Bonci, raising a pudgy little hand that half protruded from his shirt cuff, while Viterbo reached his own right hand towards the tureen without even bothering about the waiter. "These days, my digestion has been playing up. It must be the weather."

The hostess nodded understandingly, as one does with those pains in the arse who insist on telling you their ailments even when it's obvious there isn't a damned thing wrong with them.

"It must be all this humidity," Bonci went on. "I've grown accustomed to the dry heat of Turkey, and this humid, hazy climate isn't giving my stomach any rest. I was saying that to my daughter just the other day, wasn't I, Delia?"

Hearing her name, Delia Bonci raised her face from her plate and turned it towards her father.

A great poet once said that a timely silence is never appreci-ated. Well, this poet, whoever he was, could not have known Signor Bonci's daughter. Because although she remained silent, her face was decidedly eloquent. And everything in the harmony of that face, even in the composed demeanour typical of a decorous young lady on a social occasion at the beginning of the last century, conspired to express one specific thing.

Damn it, Papa, I really can't stand you.

This, at least, was the clear impression they all had. All except Signor Viterbo, who was busy devouring an extra portion of couscous, and Signor Bonci himself, who never looked at his daughter with the attention he should have.

❧

"Anyway, if you want to know why I chose this dish, well, actually it was my husband who chose it."

Secondo Gazzolo nodded placidly. "It seemed to me the most appropriate viaticum for this occasion," he said, in a slightly solemn tone. "A typically Mediterranean dish to formalise a typically Mediterranean agreement. Am I expressing it well, Signor D'Ancona?"

"Without doubt, Signor Gazzolo," Signor D'Ancona concurred at the other end of the table, placing his fork on his plate, prongs down. "There is nothing like a good meal to cement good relations between peoples."

Having said this, he looked around, as if making sure that nobody might contradict him, even if they had wanted to.

Everardo D'Ancona was a man of about seventy, with a shiny, well-groomed mane of black hair and two rows of white teeth, although very little had been seen of them up until that point: just a fleeting smile during the introductions, and a few silent displays of his open mouth as he observed the table. Nevertheless, if anyone had come into the room at that moment and asked, "Who's in charge here?" the unanimous answer would have been: "The man who just put down his fork."

"You're right," said Bonci, relaxing against the back of his chair. "When we're eating, we don't grow old. On the contrary, we preserve ourselves well. This is true throughout the world, but above all among us and our Ottoman friends. Italy and Turkey, one face one race, as you people say, Aliyan *effendi*."

"As my compatriots say," Aliyan concurred, although he did not seem enamoured of the idea that he might have the same face as Signor Bonci. "Good relations between different peoples means respecting each other's habits, traditions and culture."

"How right you are," said Mantegazza. "And the richer in traditions the two peoples are, the more difficult that is. How many more dimensions they have! In two dimensions, two straight lines on one plane will definitely meet in a point, but if they are in three dimensions, in space, it is by no means certain."

"Yes, but if they curve, they are more likely to meet," Aliyan said, looking straight ahead pensively, then turning his gaze to Bonci. "If they curve, if they curl, if they deviate from the right path, they are sure to find a meeting point, aren't they?"

Bonci was startled for a moment and appeared to stiffen very slightly. But, before he was able to ask what his fellow guest was referring to, the hostess intervened, with a linesman's sense of timing.

"The important thing, I think, is mutual respect, as Signor Aliyan said. One can also do great things in cooking by respecting another culture's habits and observing their precepts."

"Partly because they are often held in common," Artusi said, trying to retrieve the thread of a civil conversation after Signora Gazzolo had signalled offside. "For example, neither Jews nor Muslims eat pork."

"Correct," Mantegazza replied, greeting Artusi's goal kick with a decent stop, in preparation for continuing the game. "You're of Jewish origin, Signor Viterbo. Do you know why you are forbidden to eat pork?"

"It is written in Leviticus," said Viterbo, wiping his greasy chin with his napkin. "Chapter 11, verses 8 to 24."

"Yes, but that's the precept," Mantegazza observed. "Not the reason. There must be a reason why neither Jews nor Muslims touch the meat of the pig. It's the only culinary prohibition they have in common, as far as I know."

"I have sometimes reflected on that," Viterbo said, implying that this prohibition was something of a burden. "In his *Guide for the Perplexed*, Rabbi Moses Maimonides says that the pig is an unclean animal, and that nobody who has had occasion to observe how dirty pigs are will question the prohibition in any way. Basically, these animals eat their own excrement."

Mantegazza pulled a sceptical face. Rabbi Moses Maimonides, personal physician to the Caliph of Egypt and greatest philosopher of the Torah, might be authority enough for a banker who was also a believer, but not for a secular scientist.

"Yes, but that can't be the reason," the professor retorted. "Chickens and goats also feed on their own faeces, but that's no reason to prohibit their meat."

The hostess looked at Mantegazza as if wondering whether she might not have been mistaken in telling her husband to extend the invitation to him.

"That's true," Bonci observed. "Basically, the dog, too, is a domesticated animal that certainly doesn't need to be facing starvation to eat its own—"

"Excuse me, could we stop talking about such dirty things?" said Delia Bonci, looking at her father. "You're making me lose my appetite."

"Forgive us, Signorina Delia," Mantegazza said. "We doctors are so accustomed to seeing and talking about the physiological manifestations of our bodies that we sometimes fail to obey the most elementary rules of politeness. All the same, you must admit it's an interesting subject."

"Interesting, certainly, but distasteful," Aliyan retorted, showing that the word of the Qur'an was more than enough for him, although in fact he had seemed to be following the discussion quite closely.

"Not necessarily," said Artusi in a level voice. "Of course, we need to speak about digestion, but – pardon my play on words – without pushing too hard."

"In what sense, Dottore Artusi?"

Pellegrino Artusi smiled beneath his whiskers. He had said

a few times that he was not a doctor of anything, but clearly everyone at that table needed to have a title even if only out of politeness. "I think it's actually the Old Testament that comes to our rescue again. Unless I am deceiving myself, it's also Leviticus that says, 'Animals that have cloven hooves and chew the cud, these you may eat.'"

"That is so," Viterbo confirmed. "Chapter 11, verse 3."

"Then I believe the true reason lies in the chewing of the cud. Cows, goats and sheep all have rumens, stomachs subdivided into sections, that allow them to ferment the food and periodically masticate it again once it is partially digested." Artusi wondered if he should mime the gesture but decided that it was not appropriate. "The consequence of this is that the food ferments in their stomachs."

"Dottore Artusi, you assured me that we would not descend to such disgusting details," said Gazzolo, slightly embarrassed.

"We shall go no further, Signor Gazzolo." Artusi smiled reassuringly. "The fact is that in this way ruminants are able to eat grass and to draw nutrition and sustenance from it. Grass consists, principally, of a molecule called cellulose, which we use to manufacture paper. Now, we humans don't digest cellulose. We don't possess the enzymes that would break it up and so are unable to transform it into sugars."

"And what, Signor Artusi, does this have to do with the prohibition of pork?"

"Well, pigs aren't able to digest cellulose either. The pig is the best convertor of vegetable food into animal meat – but it depends on what vegetable food. If you feed it starchy foods, such as wheat, barley or maize, you get a nice, full, round pig; but if you fob it off with herbage, straw or hay, the pig definitely won't put on weight." Artusi lifted his fork, on which a morsel of meatball from the couscous had remained skewered. "By raising ruminants, the inhabitants of the Middle East were able to obtain milk and meat without having to share with them their meagre harvest of cereals. In other words, the pig was a competitor of man when it came to survival, whereas the cow or the sheep, which feeds on fodder that we don't eat, wasn't. In the struggle for the survival of the fittest, to use Darwin's phrase, the ruminant was an ally of man and the pig an enemy."

At this point Artusi would have gone on to explain that this had happened at the time of Moses (not the Moses who dealt with the Caliph of Egypt, but the one who presided over the plagues of Egypt), that times change and that the pig is in fact the best converter of carbohydrates into proteins, which explained the fairly minimal cost of pig meat, if he had not been interrupted by the host.

"The survival of the fittest, of course," Gazzolo cut in, perhaps eager to avoid the conversation going in too biological a direction. It was well known to everyone that the title of Darwin's treatise was *The Origin of Species*, which suggested that it touched on sexual matters, and Gazzolo and his wife seemed to fear that Artusi's dissertation, starting with the stomach and bypassing the intestines, might follow a consistent route southward. "Darwin's theory is extremely interesting."

"I personally find it hard to digest," said the hostess. "The idea of descending from a monkey doesn't appeal to me at all."

"Nor me," said Bonci, shaking his head. "It's all fiddlesticks."

"You're not convinced by the idea of being the relative of a chimpanzee, Bonci *effendi*?" asked Aliyan, with a sardonic smile.

"This Darwin thing isn't a theory, it's a curse," Bonci said, looking nauseated. "Anyone who has a modicum of faith in the work of the Lord knows perfectly well that these arguments about the origin of species are outrageous, sacrilegious nonsense."

Signora Clara turned slightly pale. She hadn't been able to

avoid noticing that Bonci was someone who made the sign of the cross before starting to eat, just as she certainly hadn't been able to avoid those two horrible painted wooden dummies that he had gifted to her six months earlier and that it had fallen to her to take out and put in full view in preparation for this weekend. Saint Carlo Borromeo with his right hand indicating the Trinity with thumb, index finger and middle finger, and Saint François de Sales with his stick raised, ready to bless to death anyone who didn't agree with him.

"Signor Artusi, I didn't know I had invited a dangerous Savonarola to my table," said the hostess, trying to bring a note of lightness to the discussion.

"Signora, I am merely a humble textile merchant," Artusi said calmly, feeling a blush rise to his cheeks. "In such cases, I defer to the knowledge of those who know a lot more than I do, like our mutual friend the professor. We have often discussed the theories of Darwin and his followers."

This was an attempt on Artusi's part to remind his audience – and in particular Signor D'Ancona – that he was there to gain an entrée into the market in Oriental textiles, not to discourse on heavyweight philosophies.

"I understand your dismay, Signor Bonci," said Mantegazza, trying to display greater calm than he actually possessed, "but as a university professor I can assure you that I have studied the theory of evolution in great detail, and I believe it to be the best theory we have at the moment to explain the variety and descendance of the earth's species. That certainly does not make me an unbeliever."

"Not at all," Aliyan said, shaking his head vigorously. "I'm a Muslim, I'm a believer, I bow to the ground five times a day, but I believe in evolution and its theories. In fact, it was Islam that first spoke about such things. In his *Muqaddimah*, Ibn Khaldun says that creation was a gradual process, and that life did not exist on the earth in the beginning."

"Yes, but the argument in that case was philosophical," Mantegazza said, thinking, Look at that, the Arabs always believe they invented something themselves. Whatever it might be, from mathematics to cooking, they always did it first. "Darwin's theory is a scientific theory, based on observation and deduction. I have studied it carefully, as I said, and at the moment there is no evidence to refute its veracity, as far as I know."

Mantegazza looked around him, welcoming the manifest approval of D'Ancona and other guests.

But Bonci obviously had no intention of throwing in the towel. He turned to Mantegazza with a honeyed smile. "As far as you know. Precisely. Forgive me, Professore Mantegazza, but I think it unlikely that you know more than the good Lord who created us, wouldn't you agree?"

"Definitely less than Him, Signor Bonci, but just as definitely more than you," the Turk commented, still with that smile that made you want to slap him. "Forgive my honesty, Bonci *effendi*. Seeing that you are such a fervent Catholic, you should have no difficulty in doing so."

Bonci's face turned even redder, either from the effect of the Turk's words, or because at these words his daughter had started to yawn, exactly like someone trying to restrain laughter.

It was at that moment, fortunately, that Bartolomeo entered and announced in a solemn tone:

"Ladies and gentlemen, the dessert."

Which was served, and consumed, in religious silence.

Minus 1

"Yes, 1820," Mantegazza replied, looking up and nodding slowly. "Whereas I was born in 1830, like you, if I understood correctly."

"Exactly," said Signor D'Ancona, also nodding as he buttoned up his waistcoat with a slow but firm hand. "We're exactly the same age. It wouldn't seem so, would it?"

The professor's face remained impassive, although inside himself he was shaking his head vigorously.

Mantegazza had just finished his examination of D'Ancona, who after lunch had mentioned his own respiratory troubles and had asked him for advice. Like every self-respecting doctor, Mantegazza was a doctor even before being a human being, and he had therefore taken D'Ancona, stretched him out on the bed and so on. D'Ancona had been stripped, examined, manipulated; now, after all these past participles, came the moment for the diagnosis. A cold, perhaps a touch of bronchitis. So: no fire in the room – the fumes would irritate the bronchial tubes – but instead, a nice bed warmer under the blankets and tomorrow you'll be in better shape than before. It wouldn't take much, because generally speaking – Mantegazza didn't say this out loud – you're not exactly a picture of health.

"You seem to me in excellent form," Mantegazza lied. "It might perhaps be advisable for you to spend more time in the open air. I spent my younger years in the forests of the Amazon. That's the kind of thing that toughens you up."

"Yes, and I grew up on a farm," D'Ancona said. "But I've been cooped up behind a desk since I was a young man. It was my destiny, obviously. And gradually I've lost certain abilities."

"Physically, perhaps," said Mantegazza, unconsciously steering the conversation towards his speciality: a lecture on geriatrics, complete with questions and answers. "But mentally, I'd wager you're better than the young man you were. The body's faculties start to dwindle when those of the mind are still to be developed, did you know that?"

"Are you saying that as a doctor or as a priest?" D'Ancona asked, smiling. "Are you saying it to treat me or to console me?"

"For heaven's sake, priests should be called to hospitals only for extreme unction," Mantegazza replied. At a pinch, the nuns can sometimes be useful, he thought, but did not say. "Far be it from me to wish to console you. No, my dear Signor D'Ancona, the senses and the body abandon us before the mind."

"And what sense abandons us first as we advance in age?"

"There isn't a ranking as such. There are those who lose their sight first, others their hearing."

"Ah, if truth be told, the only one practically remaining to me is touch."

"Touch, from the Latin *tactus*, also the origin of the word 'tact'. I'd say that given the diplomatic nature of your work, it's the only sense you can't do without. Your Ottoman colleague might need to work on his a little."

"Aliyan is still young, the lucky fellow. He's hot-blooded, in every sense of the term. He will learn. As for me, though, there are abilities I cannot learn again. Some, anyway."

D'Ancona pointed to his spectacles, silver frames enclosing two ellipses, small and narrow, but thick as the soles of a boot. If the lenses had been of normal dimensions, the spectacles would have been a lot heavier.

"At least one can improve one's sight. These new lenses have

allowed me to see things that previously I could only remember."
D'Ancona sighed. "But other things might get a lot worse. Is it possible, for example, to lose the sense of taste?"

"Oh, in principle, of course. But I believe it can only happen *in extrema ratio*."

"Has it ever happened to any of your patients?"

"No, not as far as I know."

D'Ancona laughed.

"It's no laughing matter, you know. When it comes down to it, taste is one of the most useful and satisfying senses, especially at our age."

"No, forgive me. You were referring before to Signor Aliyan, but just now I was thinking of your friend Signor Artusi. For him it would be a terrible misfortune."

"I can fully reassure you on that count. In Signor Artusi, all five senses are in perfect working order." Mantegazza touched his temple. "Even the board of directors on the top floor, you know, is fully active."

"I was made well aware of that at lunch today," D'Ancona said. "The speech he made at table about Hebrew customs certainly impressed me."

⁓

"For heaven's sake," said Artusi. "It was simply an argument dictated by common sense. A merchant's argument, that's what it was."

"And that's just what we need, Artusi *effendi*," Aliyan replied, opening his hands as if demonstrating an obvious truth. "Merchants, not philosophers or theoreticians. Right now, my country is in difficulties. We need to move to stay afloat, otherwise we will drown."

"To move as much as that, what's needed is young people like you, Signor Aliyan."

Artusi expected the Turk to rise to his full height, aware of the role with which History had invested him. Instead, he shook his head, doubtfully. "And to learn to swim, we need swimming teachers, Artusi *effendi*." Aliyan moved his hands back and forth, beating the air. "Dogs can swim without anyone teaching them, but not men. I attended military school at Manastir, then the Sisli military academy in Istanbul. We learned how to organise an army from you. Before a regular army, we had the Janissaries, who had seized power. We trained a proper army, and we set it to guard the Sublime Porte."

"I understand. Now you want to train merchants."

"Nobody trades better than we Levantines when it's a matter of dealing in small quantities." Aliyan made a gesture similar to that of preparing a package, whatever that meant. "But as I learned in the army, it's one thing to move one person, another thing to move a hundred, and quite another to move a thousand. And there are more than thirty million of us. We're a huge market, and we need people who have a wider view. Like you, Artusi *effendi*."

Pellegrino Artusi spread his whiskers a little, giving them the shape of a narrow smile, the kind that comes spontaneously to polite people when others start to flatter them. And, as Artusi knew perfectly well, when the other party butters you up, he often does so the better to extract something from you.

"It's just a matter of experience, Signor Aliyan. I've been cheated so many times, I've learned when to trust someone and when not to."

"When one has a wagon filled with silk, Artusi *effendi*, being cheated is an experience. When one has an empire, being cheated is a pestilence. One cannot wait to discover it, one must see it first. From the numbers, from the proceeds, from the accounts." Aliyan made the gesture of running through figures on a sheet of paper. "You're a skilful merchant, who understands many things. Do you also understand about financial audits?"

Artusi half closed his eyes, somewhat pensive. So this was what the Turk had been leading up to. Checking the accounts. But a particular account, or accounts in general?

"A little, Signor Aliyan. Perhaps not enough for what you're talking about. I can give you my opinion as a merchant, but I don't know how useful I could be to you as an accountant. Signor Bonci, for example, may be sanctimonious, but he seems to be an expert in his field and no doubt knows the Ottoman market better than I, having lived among you for a long period of time."

Silence.

If lunch had not sufficed, the fact that a passing mention of Bonci should be enough to silence the Turk was further confirmation that there was no love lost between the two men.

After a few seconds' embarrassment, it struck Artusi that it might be best to change the subject. "Talking of expert opinions, did you like the *cuscussù* at lunch today? It's a dish from your part of the world, if I understood correctly."

"Not exactly. We have different tastes, we and the Italians. Things that you think very tasty seem bland to us."

"Yes, I've had occasion to note that," Artusi replied, remembering the over-spiced beef produced by Gazzolo. "I know Signor Gazzolo's canned meat has met with your approval."

"Indeed it has. Gazzolo's company produces various kinds of canned food, but as far as I know that type of meat is produced exclusively for us. The taste is probably too strong for the Italians."

"I fear that is indeed the case," Artusi confirmed. "But I should imagine there are tastes our two peoples would have in common.

Indeed, you, who know both Italy and Turkey, might be able to tell me of a few."

Aliyan nodded vigorously and somewhat presumptuously. "More than one, in fact. Our cuisine is very rich, Signor Artusi, and a thousand years old."

As if ours isn't. But Pellegrino wasn't interested so much in arguing as in the concrete possibility of extending even further his collection of recipes. "And what would you consider the best of them?"

"There is a dish typical of my country that Italians and Europeans always like very much. It's called *meze*. I don't know how to translate that."

"*Meze*? When is it eaten? At the beginning of a meal, at the end?"

"No, no. It can be eaten at any time, although not as a dessert."

"Then I imagine it as something light, to be served between the main courses. How is it prepared?"

"You need peppers and walnuts, before anything else. But it's hard to explain, I really would have to show you. Once one has the ingredients, it can be made in a short time. But right now, I must confer with D'Ancona *effendi*, and at seven dinner will be served. And tomorrow morning we will leave before ten."

"I understand. Don't worry. I, too, will be leaving early. I was planning to wake up at my usual hour, no later than five."

We've thrown the bait, now let's wait for the carp to bite. You can't tell a military man who's younger than you and clearly vain that you wake up well before he does without wounding his pride.

Aliyan stopped to think, his pupils darting here and there very rapidly if almost imperceptibly, as if searching in his brain for a solution. "Wait. Could you get up at five?"

"I do so every morning." Artusi lied again, really laying it on thick.

"As I was saying, once one has the ingredients, it can be made in a short time." Aliyan smiled. "If you like, tomorrow morning before breakfast we could throw together a short lesson in Ottoman cuisine."

"I would be pleased and honoured, Signor Aliyan," replied Artusi, smiling in his turn.

Basically, this Turk, too, seemed like a good person.

~~~

"He's a pain in the arse, my dear Bartolomeo."

Behind Gazzolo, Bartolomeo nodded deferentially. The same term that, if used by Crocetta, would have led to serious consequences on the personal and professional level, caused him absolutely no bother when said by the master – he was the master, after all, and why on earth shouldn't he have the perfect right to express himself as he wished in his own house?

"It did indeed strike me that Signor Aliyan is a trifle pretentious, sir," said Bartolomeo, putting down the wheelbarrow with the buckets and opening the door to Signor Gazzolo – who had actually been in front of him a moment before, so that in order to open the door wide a somewhat complicated movement had been necessary, more typical of a centre forward than of a butler.

"More than a trifle," Secondo Gazzolo said, nodding towards the two buckets. "So, the guinea fowl go in the kitchen, and then we have to go down to the cellar for the wine."

"I'll see to it immediately," replied Bartolomeo.

"Thank you, Bartolomeo. You go and get the wine, I'll see to the guinea fowl."

"It's a heavy load, sir," Bartolomeo observed, his tone a mixture of anxiety and disapproval. Indeed, the large metal bucket contained half a dozen frozen guinea fowl, conserved in dry ice, and must have weighed no less than 20 kilos. Not to mention the fact that carrying heavy loads was certainly not a dignified thing for the master of the house to do. What on earth would the other guests think if they saw the master of the house himself transporting weights? They would be sure to conclude that the butler was neither reliable nor worthy of his role.

"I'll manage it easily, Bartolomeo, don't worry," Gazzolo said curtly. Bartolomeo was a jewel of a butler, but he was of the belief that his employer had no hands and that rich people must all be like that deadbeat Conte Pepoli, who got out of breath stirring his soup with a spoon.

"It may be more appropriate if I see to it, sir," replied Bartolomeo. "The guests might think it unbecoming for you to occupy yourself personally with the provisions."

Gazzolo nodded slowly, scratching his beard. "Yes, you may be right. Now you know where to put them, don't you?"

Bartolomeo emitted the cry of the embarrassed butler, a brief outburst of coughing, before replying in a respectful but firm manner. Being a control freak was all well and good, but this was an exaggeration. "If I may be so bold, sir, I have been living in this house since 1850. I am sure I can find both the kitchen and the cellar, as well as the other rooms of the house."

"All right," said Gazzolo, unbuttoning his coat. "As regards what we were talking about earlier, there was a little friction between Signor Aliyan and Signor Bonci at lunch today."

"I did notice a certain tension between the lunch guests, sir," Bartolomeo commented, without adding anything that might reveal a particular preference of his. True, Aliyan was insufferable, but Bonci was also a poke in the eye.

"At dinner, I need the service to be rapid," said Gazzolo, as Bartolomeo was closing the door, "so that we can get everyone up as soon as possible. After dinner, I'll try to keep the two of them separated. I don't want any more unpleasant situations, especially not involving the Turk. We need to keep him sweet."

"What about accompanying the gentlemen to their rooms?"

"No problem. I've noticed that, whenever possible, Aliyan clings to D'Ancona as if he were mother duck." Gazzolo started to take off his coat, much to the regret of Bartolomeo who was watching him from behind and thinking: What's the point of having a butler if you dress and undress by yourself? "I'll pretend to be concerned about Signor D'Ancona's health and accompany them both to their rooms, first one and then the other."

"Bonci's and Aliyan's rooms are close to each other," Bartolomeo replied after a moment's thought. "So I could take the other guests, making sure I took Bonci first, to show that we really care about his comfort. Then if you'd be kind enough to wait for me before accompanying the second group of guests, I'll be able to avoid further embarrassment."

Servile, yes, but efficient, dear old Bartolomeo. Gazzolo nodded his approval.

"Good, good. For now, everything is sorted. We'll serve tea when the guests come back, but there's no hurry. Aliyan's outside with Artusi, Bonci's out and about somewhere with old Viterbo, the man who holds the purse strings. The professor's with D'Ancona in his room. I don't think I've forgotten anyone."

"Just Signorina Delia Bonci."

"Oh, yes, the slyboots," said Gazzolo. "Who knows? Maybe she's in her room."

~※~

Delia Bonci was indeed in her room. Alone, and locked in – and the hand that had turned the key was not hers. Given that Bartolomeo would never have allowed himself to shut a guest in his or her room, the only other person who could possibly be responsible was her father. A father who had been hit very hard by the laughter that had escaped his daughter at lunch, and had retaliated by hitting her very hard, on the left cheek. After which he had closed the door and locked it.

This was unnecessary, however, because at that point Delia Bonci would not even have dreamed of going out and seeing anybody. All she wanted was to be alone, without anybody to see her cry, in fact without anybody to see her. Alone, in the dark, waiting.

Waiting for dinnertime to come, when she would have to go out and present herself at table.

Waiting, later, for that banker, a man as fat as a pig, to ask her father for her hand in marriage.

Waiting, even later, for the same banker, now her husband, to return home, and not knowing if she hoped for him to return or not.

Waiting to have to do something.

A terrible fate, being a woman.

"If we women didn't deal with it, my dear Crocetta, the world would be in a mess, that's for sure."

On her feet in the drawing room, Signora Clara Gazzolo was watching as Crocetta shifted a heavy-looking armchair into the centre of the room. Very soon, the guests would all be returning for a nice tea with *crostate*: the best way to recover from the biting wind outside and get in the right mood for dinner two hours later. A serious matter, nothing like the pre-dinner aperitifs we poor twenty-first-century amateurs make do with.

"No, move that one a little more to the right," Signora Clara said, gesturing with the back of her hand. "It's the only one that Signor Viterbo can fit into, and Signor Viterbo has to sit there, a long way from the table with the sweets."

"You mean otherwise he'll finish all of them?"

"Don't let my husband hear you make one of your comments when the guests are around, Crocetta. Men have no sense of humour, at least not when they're being talked about." Signora Clara sighed. "If Signor Viterbo sits there, then Signorina Delia will have to sit here, which means Signor Bonci will end up there."

"In other words, a long way from the Turk. I understand."

"At least you understand me straight away. I had to explain it to Secondo. 'Those two hate each other,' I told him. 'If you want to continue making sure these meetings take place in your house, you have to use a little diplomacy. A little savoir faire.'" Signora Clara opened her hands, as if serving platitudes on a platter. "Like that business with the bishops. Every time Bonci comes here, I have to remember to take out those two horrible wooden dolls and put them in the drawing room. I think there's a reason people give tea services as presents. And Bonci's so touchy, oh my God, yes. Anyway, I was telling Secondo, 'You have to take care of these things. Otherwise, the next time our dear D'Ancona will move bag and baggage to Viterbo's house.'"

"And what did he say?"

"Oh, my dear. At first he hardly listened to me, you know what men are like."

Of course Crocetta does. A head, two legs, two arms and eight hands. God made me ugly, but they're all over me anyway. Just imagine if I was pretty.

"At the very least he was thinking of something else. Then after a while he said, 'Thank you, my dear, you did well,' and sent for Bartolomeo." Signora Clara sighed, conscious of her own role in the world. "It takes a woman, my dear Crocetta, to think of certain things."

~☩~

"Of course, it takes a woman, Signor Viterbo. Especially at your age, trust me."

"That's precisely what holds me back, you know, Signor Bonci," said Corrado Viterbo, gently shaking the ash from a cigar as wide as his thumb. "I'm almost sixty. I'm no longer a lad, as you've just reminded me."

"Ours is the best age, my dear Signor Viterbo," Bonci retorted. "We're no longer children, but we're not yet old. And you're a person who's held in high esteem, trust me. You're bound to have many suitors, and after all, it's been several years."

Indeed, it had been several years.

Five years, to be precise, since his beloved Eunice had succumbed to tuberculosis and passed away. Five years spent alone, without a wife or children – they had never had any – and devoting ever more of his time to work and food, the only two things that consoled him.

"Yes, it's been several years," Bonci repeated.

And then Delia had arrived, young Delia. Bringing him the accounts and contracts from her father's company every Wednesday. And Corrado Viterbo had found himself waiting for those Wednesdays with an increasing sense of anticipation.

Waiting for young Delia to arrive.

With that polite manner of hers. That sulky little face.

"I think the moment has come, my dear Corrado – if you'll allow me to call you by your Christian name – to make your choice."

And that insufferable father.

Insufferable.

Papa's insufferable.

Delia was looking out of the window without seeing anything. Outside, the wind was whistling, but Delia didn't hear it. The only thing she was conscious of was that Papa was a horrible person. Just as this place was horrible. Just as her house was horrible. Everywhere that Papa was, was horrible.

No matter if it was a fine townhouse, like the one where she lived, or a castle like this. Even a courtyard would be all right if he weren't there. Well, maybe not a courtyard. A little house maybe. But alone. That is, no, not exactly alone. But not with that hot air balloon in tails her father wanted her to marry.

Still looking out, she saw Secondo Gazzolo walking along, keeping close to the wall of the castle, holding a large crate and another object she couldn't make out. He stopped just below Delia's window, took a kind of wooden peg from behind the hedge and inserted it in a crack in the wall.

Behind that wall, Delia had the impression that a door opened.

Gazzolo placed a hand on the door and opened it. But, before entering, he took the indistinguishable object that he had in his hand, put it on his head and pulled it down over his face. An object that Delia had never seen up close, but which at that point she recognised easily.

It was a fencing mask.

From the diary of Pellegrino Artusi

Campoventoso, 16 October, 1900

I open these pages at a late hour, an unwonted one, I think: it is almost five in the morning, and I have only just got back to my room.

This evening, or I should say yesterday evening, after dinner, Gazzolo accompanied me, Viterbo, the Turk and Signor D'Ancona to our rooms. He delivered Aliyan first, followed by D'Ancona, and both of them locked themselves in their rooms; this surprised me somewhat, but on reflection it occurred to me that both these gentlemen must have documents of some importance in their rooms, and perhaps also a certain amount of money, and assuming the habit of locking one's door is sensible when one is in someone else's house, and sometimes, depending on the domestics one has, in one's own house too.

Having left Signor D'Ancona in his room, Gazzolo told us that he did not feel at all sleepy, and that once he had seen us to our rooms he would go off and play a game of billiards, his favourite pastime on his many sleepless nights. As I, too, felt alert and lively, I offered to keep him company, and Viterbo also announced that he was in no way desirous of crawling under the blankets. So, having dismissed the butler, who had been with us until that moment, we made our way to the ground floor.

And so we started playing billiards, which is always a good excuse for a little chat. In fact, my good father always said he did not trust anyone who played in silence.

Gazzolo first placed a bottle of rum and some glasses next to the billiard table and invited us to help ourselves, since he certainly could not disturb the butler at that late hour; Viterbo took him at his word, filling his own glass generously more than once, his expression affable but not serene, which made me certain that he was somewhat out of sorts.

At first, I misunderstood the nature of his distress, given that I had seen with my own eyes how Viterbo ate rather with a spade than with a spoon. He had in addition been served a timbale of cauliflower, which is notorious for causing flatulence. I therefore took the liberty of remarking to him that, if his problem was excessive pressure on the abdomen, it might be best to give nature free rein – after all, only men were present – than to introduce more material suitable for fermentation, such as alcohol.

Viterbo told me, laughing only from his nose down, that he had no problems with his stomach, which made Gazzolo observe that in that case the source of the problem must lie somewhat higher up.

~≈~

Viterbo hedged at first, but Gazzolo is not the type of person to be fobbed off with a statement that black is white; in addition, rum is certainly not a beverage that strengthens willpower; so that after a while Viterbo heaved a deep sigh and said: "The truth is, I have been asking myself whether or not I am too old to get married. Or rather, since we are here, I am asking you."

~≈~

I remained silent, from a sense of decency. I have managed to reach the age of eighty without marrying, despite having robust natural inclinations towards the fairer sex, or rather, precisely because of that. But I know that my temperament is a particular one and that not everyone feels like me. Fortunately, the master of the house saw to it that I was saved embarrassment. "The one piece of advice I can give you," Gazzolo said to him, "is to keep away from marriage brokers, who combine the arranging of unions with monetary reward," and I could not help but agree.

I remember when, both my parents having died, I was left with two sisters who were starting to advance in years and longed to find husbands. Anyone who has known what it is to have old maids in the house will concur with me as to what a torment it is having to tolerate them. I began therefore with the financial aspect, which is usually the persuasive argument, increased the dowry off my own bat by a thousand francesconi and called in the marriage brokers.

If only I had never done so.

People came to the house whom one would have liked to flee from, or to kick out of the door, or both, in whichever order. I remember a fellow named Buccianti, from Navacchio near Pisa, a grain and fertiliser merchant, who told me he could read numbers but not letters, and that he needed a woman in the house who could read contracts to him and stop him from being cheated. Imagining one of my sisters married to such a yokel made my blood boil and, although I tried to suppress my anger, the marriage broker himself became aware of it and rushed to the door, taking the bumpkin with him, before I could open my mouth. To cut a long story short, I managed to marry them both off in the end but had to do so all by myself.

Viterbo answered these arguments by stating that it was not his intention to entrust himself to a wife trader, and that in reality he had his eyes on a pretty, well-mannered young woman who seemed to fit the bill perfectly. What held him back, he said, was that he felt he might be too distant, in age and other things, from the young lady in question.

Thus it was that, while Viterbo spoke, I was reminded of the case of poor Domenico.

⌘

Domenico was known as Mengone, since he was Herculean in physique: in Emilia-Romagna, Domenico is shortened to Mengo, which then becomes Mengone if he is tall and strong, or Menghino if he is of laughable proportions. This Domenico had no time for those who celebrated Mass on Sundays, and having grown up in a Papal state, he got into so much trouble that he was obliged to find refuge in England, where, since he was an efficient steward, he easily found service with important nobles. But while he was in England, he met a beautiful young Irishwoman who in religion was not just Catholic, but ultra-Catholic, who became engaged to a liberal Mengone and eventually married, in church, a Domenico converted to the Mass and all that went with it. Of the honest, open-minded young man, there was no longer any trace. As he got older, things became even worse, and the Mengone I met again in Italy after many years was more Papist than the Pope.

I told this story, and we began to discuss it. Gazzolo, who is the kind of man who, although of a fine mind, demonstrates a certain vulgarity when he finds himself in male company, commented by saying that a single hair from a woman's pussy has more pulling power than a pair of oxen. I did not agree and explained why.

I have seen a great many of those anticlerical liberals of '31 who finished their days serving Mass and carrying the canopy;

I have known them as bachelors and as married men. When one is young, one has a generous heart overflowing with love of one's country, and one often lets oneself be drawn into enterprises that are not always legal; but once the passions have cooled, they are often replaced by remorse, especially in those who, of a benign heart and little education, do not have deep convictions. They were liberals when they were young, to satisfy their impulses for freedom; they become Bible-thumpers when they are more mature, to satisfy their impulses for peace and quiet. They follow their instincts, as if they were not men, but quadrupeds.

As I said this, I saw Viterbo nodding and looking at me with what, if I am not mistaken, I understood as renewed esteem.

❧

I think I grasped the fact that Viterbo's anxiety has two voices: one whispers in his ear that he is too old to marry again, and the other reminds him that he is Jewish, and that the young lady he would like to wed is a Gentile. In fact, I have become convinced, as would anyone with eyes in his head, that the candidate for title of the future Signora Viterbo is none other than young Delia Bonci. And if that is the case, the good banker's reservations are understandable: if you want your children to be Jewish, says the Torah, their mother must be Jewish; one always knows who the mother is, as the Talmudic laws state, not without a certain pragmatism. And what we saw today at lunch tells me, with certainty, that young Delia and, above all, her father are quite Catholic. Now, one may become Catholic, but not, it appears, Jewish; one would have to be reborn. And if one could even decide how and where to be reborn, I am almost certain that one would choose to change quite other things in one's life than one's ethnicity, whatever that is.

But these are the ramblings of an old man made gaga by lack of sleep, and it is only now that I realise how many pages I have filled. It will be best to finish here, since Aliyan is waiting for me, ready to teach me how to cook a new dish. Awake all night, and now I am getting ready to begin the morning with peppers: let us hope for the best!

1

Calmly but cautiously, Bartolomeo walked along the corridor to the north of the castle's piano nobile.

And as he walked, he ticked off from his mental list the tasks he had just carried out. Even though it was an early hour, he had already done a considerable number of things.

Supervise the serving of breakfast: done. Inspect and instruct the waiters: done. Write in a fine hand the lunch menu for the guests who would be remaining: done. Check that the carriages were clean and tidy for the guests who were leaving: done.

And then there were the tasks that remained to be completed.

Around him, in the half-light of dawn – it was six in the morning – the friendly tapestries were kind enough to muffle the already stealthy sound of his footsteps.

A small yawn spread across the butler's features. He had been awake all night, playing canasta with the cook and the estate manager, as he did every Saturday. And he had even won a tidy amount. But the worries remained. This was not a Sunday like any other.

There was nobody in the rest of the corridor, and the only sound came from the inside of his trousers, which rustled at every step, something Bartolomeo would only have been able to avoid by walking like a cowboy – which would have been quite unbecoming to the butler of a grand house.

Throughout that floor, in short, silence reigned.

A silence that was broad, calm and deep.

And yet not completely reassuring.

In that silence, something was missing.

"Are we nearly there?"

Artusi's question had been a brief one, not so much from a lack of politeness as from a lack of breath. For at least ten minutes now, he had been following Aliyan, who after wishing him good morning had set off with long – very long – and nimble strides in the direction of the castle's olive grove, a good kilometre away.

Artusi and Aliyan had met in the kitchen at 5.30 for a quick coffee, then, after a brief exchange of pleasantries, had left the castle and set off for the olive grove.

Actually, both men would have liked to linger in the warmth of the kitchen: but the cook, a virago of indefinable age, had politely observed that it was up to her to feed the guests, that there was a lot of work to do and not much space in there to move about, and that if the gentlemen wanted to play with pots and pans, there was a good outdoor stove in the olive grove, the kind used for roasting chestnuts.

And so the two of them had left the castle. Aliyan had the ingredients with him in a small bag – apart from the final one, which was to be plucked directly from the tree.

"Which is right behind the olive grove, Artusi *effendi*. We've been lucky."

Pellegrino Artusi did not reply. The two of them had agreed, it was true, that the Turk would cook while Artusi would help, observe, and above all write. This had seemed a good idea to Artusi a dozen hours earlier. But none of those hours had been spent sleeping, and right now, with his eyes swollen with sleep and his lungs up between his ears, it didn't seem quite such a good idea.

"We are almost there, *effendi*. There, behind that line of trees."

And there indeed it was: a small bush, almost adolescent in the midst of so many rough old olive trees. The pomegranate, born of the blood of Dionysus, with whose seeds Hades bound Persephone to him for half of eternity. Artusi would have said this if he had had sufficient breath. Given the condition of his lungs, he confined himself to simply nodding.

"October, the best month," the Turk said. "The seeds are the best of the season, ripe but still sour. And there's the stove."

"Is it best to light it immediately?"

"No, we don't need the embers, we just need the fire." Aliyan pointed to an area towards the bottom of the bush, some fifty centimetres from the ground, where a dozen promising fruits swayed in the wind. "Now the thing to do is pick the pomegranates and take the seeds. We already have the walnuts, we just need to shell them."

"Then why don't you pick the pomegranates, while I shell the walnuts?"

You've made me trek all the way here, you're surely not expecting me to bend over that bush, are you? I'm already on the verge of a heart attack, which would be a painful death in itself, all I need now is to put my back out and we're done.

～※～

"Everything done, Bartolomeo?"

"Please lower your voice, Crocetta. Some of the guests are still asleep."

"But they're all over in *that* part. Here in the west they're all awake."

"Not all of them. Signor D'Ancona isn't up yet."

Crocetta looked sceptically at Bartolomeo. "Is he still asleep?"

"So it would seem."

"That's a bit strange, don't you think?"

Bartolomeo nodded, more with his eyes than with his head. "He's usually an early riser."

Actually, both Bartolomeo and Crocetta were thinking the same thing: that if Signor D'Ancona really was asleep, then the silence in the corridor was truly strange. In normal circumstances, Signor D'Ancona snored like a mill with rocks inside; that was why Bartolomeo and Crocetta, on the weekends when he was a guest, never put anyone in the room next to his. It would have been like trying to sleep in the middle of the fans' stand in a football stadium. And that was when he was in good health; with a cold, it was unlikely things would improve.

Despite this, there was no sound in the corridor at that moment. And even right next to the door of Signor D'Ancona's room, which was where the two servants were, nothing could be heard.

"Do you think he's sick?"

"I wouldn't rule out the possibility."

"Maybe we ought to knock."

"Signor D'Ancona hasn't expressed such a desire," said Bartolomeo, coldly.

"I don't think he's expressed the desire to feel sick either, but sometimes things happen even though the butler hasn't been asked, don't you think?"

Ice formed on the butler's highest slopes. "We'll talk later about this impertinence of yours," he said, raising his gloved left hand in a clenched fist (to knock at the door, you didn't think he was going to hit her, did you?).

Discreetly, Bartolomeo rapped three times on the door.

There was no answer.

Three more discreet raps.

There was no answer.

Bartolomeo prepared his fist again and Crocetta glared at

him. It's stupid to do the same thing several times and expect a different result, her eyes said.

What else can we do? Bartolomeo's eyebrows asked.

Move out of the way, Crocetta's pupils ordered.

She bent down and placed her right eye against the keyhole.

"I think it'd be best to call the doctor, Bartolomeo," she said in a low voice, even before she rose again.

"Shouldn't we inform the master first?"

"You're right, Bartolomeo. You go and tell Signor Gazzolo, and I'll go down to the breakfast room and fetch the—"

"Please," Bartolomeo interrupted her, raising his hand. "The upstairs maid entering the dining room! Accidents may happen, but there's a limit to everything."

᠂ᢦᢞᡄ᠊

"Professore . . ."

Mantegazza, his face and goatee inclined in the direction of a magnificent plate of bacon and eggs, looked up at the butler. The only professor of anything in that room was him.

"What is it?"

"Your presence is requested upstairs, Professore."

Bartolomeo had emphasised the word "Professore" not so much to avoid ambiguity, as not to call Mantegazza "Dottore" and therefore avoid alarming anyone needlessly. It is well known that a doctor is often requested in conditions of emergency, while a professor is consulted in order to get an informed opinion and prevent such emergencies from happening. At least, this is how it was a century ago.

"I understand."

After a rapid glance at his plate, Mantegazza looked at the butler, who was still by his side.

A pearl of a butler. One who would never have brought a request to a person having his breakfast in peace if it had not been for something damnably urgent.

Forget about professor. What was needed here was a doctor. If need be, I can get the eggs cooked again later.

"All right, Bartolomeo. Show me the way."

❧

"He's dead, Signor Gazzolo. He's been dead for several hours."

Standing by the bed, Mantegazza let go of Signor D'Ancona's wrist, with a gentleness rendered necessary more by the context than by anything else.

Facing him, Secondo Gazzolo, still in his country clothes, since the news had reached him while he was on the farm for his usual inspection of the animals: true, it was Sunday morning, but when a cow has to give birth, she doesn't do it during working hours.

At the door, Bartolomeo, who had remained there after opening it with the passkey, stood with his hands behind his back, looking drained. Looking just as drained was Gazzolo. The poor man hadn't slept: he had been up all night, and then the estate manager had come to fetch him at five o'clock for the morning round.

"Then we couldn't have done anything. Even if we'd arrived earlier."

"No, I fear not. Death occurred several hours ago. At least four, perhaps more."

"I see." Gazzolo hesitated. "I knew he was of delicate health, and he did look rather tired yesterday, but we're never prepared, are we, Professore?"

Mantegazza didn't reply immediately. At that moment, as

already said, he didn't feel like a professor, but a doctor. And one of the undeniable characteristics of doctors is that they are usually rather ready to put on the mental white coat of their profession. Even in the worst situations, going from a hot dish to a cold body.

"I need a favour, my dear Gazzolo."

"I fear there will be many favours asked of me today. Tell me."

"Could you get some sturdy grooms to move the body to a more appropriate place?"

"But of course. Bartolomeo, call Dante and tell him to come here with Troccolo and a pair of poles."

The butler bowed his head in consent and left the room.

"Yes, it's a consideration I should have thought of. We must take him a long way from where the guests are. You have experience of these things. Where do you think would be best?"

"Basically, somewhere where there's light. I need to examine him properly."

"Examine him properly? But my dear professor, you said yourself that the poor man is dead . . ."

Mantegazza kept his eyes on the corpse. It was Gazzolo's heavy, forced breathing that told him the master of the house had got the point.

Because D'Ancona was dead, but when Mantegazza had last seen him, he had still been alive. He had even examined him.

And the man hadn't died because of a heart attack or an apoplectic fit.

"I can't say anything before examining the body thoroughly, my dear Secondo."

But in my opinion, this fellow was suffocated.

⚜

Yes, we suffocate.

In big cities, we suffocate.

Too many people, too little space.

Pellegrino Artusi took a deep breath, enjoying one of a human being's most elementary duties, even before eating and sleeping.

Breathing. It is so vital and yet we pay so little attention to it. We only become aware of it when we are out of breath, for whatever reason. Now, Artusi didn't often have difficulty breathing in everyday life: he was a calm man, not given to anxiety, and his advanced age prevented those activities which usually lead to breathlessness, both those with our trousers on and those with them off. That was why he was now enjoying his own breathing, which was once again clear, regular and deep.

Men need air. Morning air, particularly. It's fresh, it's new. It restores you to the world.

Artusi looked at the table, where all the ingredients were ready to be cooked. The peppers, the walnuts, the pomegranate juice, the oil and the bread. All that was missing was the fire.

It wasn't until they were about to light the stove that Aliyan and Artusi had realised that there was no firewood, either inside the thing or round about; at that point Aliyan had said that he would go and fetch some from the castle.

"The kitchens will be even busier at this hour, and I wouldn't like you to get into trouble like I did," Artusi had said, his chest and hands covered in dark stains: the kind of thing that happens when you have to squeeze pomegranate seeds and the only utensils at your disposal are two hands and a lot of goodwill.

Aliyan stopped to think for a moment. "I don't think it'll be necessary to go to the kitchen."

"Do you need a helping hand?" Artusi asked, in the devious tone of someone implying that if you can't carry a dozen kilos of firewood on your own you are a slowcoach and probably also a bit of a pansy.

"I'm grateful, but I can do it by myself," the Turk assured him, conscious that if his cooking companion had developed emphysema because of a ten-minute walk wearing only an overcoat, he might well end up a dead man doing the same walk backwards and forwards with a few kilos of firewood.

Actually, another dead man. But Aliyan couldn't know that.

⸙

So Artusi had remained alone, happy and calm. *Beata solitudo, sola beatitudo.* Of course, it depends. If you choose it, solitude is wonderful. As long as it's short. Everything is tiresome if it goes on too long. Which meant . . .

Which meant, as Artusi had long since realised, although he regretted not having understood it earlier, that the important thing is change. Our senses get used to things if they are always exposed to the same stimuli. And so there are two possible conclusions: either we give them more, or we have to give them something different.

And if you give them more, sooner or later you'll have had enough. Change, of course, but at the right rhythm, and in the right things. It's not that you have to start to walk with your head down. But nor should you spend your whole life eating nothing but pasta with tomato sauce.

While Artusi was absorbed in his own thoughts, he saw Aliyan approaching from a distance with two bundles of logs under his armpits, at the nimble pace of someone who knows where he's going.

"Here we are," said the Turk, dropping his load in front of the stove. "There was no need to go to the kitchen."

"Good," said Artusi, stirring himself. "I think we can light the fire now. I already have a bit of an appetite, I must say."

"Yes, so have I."

Artusi looked at his cooking companion with a conspiratorial air. "Listen, do we need the full fire, or could we make do with the embers?"

Aliyan looked in the direction of the castle, then turned towards Pellegrino. "Perhaps the embers might be best."

"Very good. Then I suggest we light the stove and then go back to the castle and have breakfast. When the fire's down to the embers, we'll come back here and put the pot on."

Because solitude is a good thing, fresh air is a good thing, but I'm hungry and it's getting windier here. Excellent for fires, but very bad for Artusi.

So Aliyan formed a pyramid of logs while Artusi crumpled a few sheets of yellow paper and handed them to the Turk.

"We need more," said Aliyan, who had taken command of operations in a military manner, so that there was no need to bend down.

"Do you think so? With this wind, two or three sheets should be quite enough."

"Yes, but the firewood is damp. Damp and cold. We mustn't hold back. Do we still have paper?"

"We're in the middle of a negotiation with an official organ of the Kingdom of Italy," said Artusi, smiling and taking more sheets. "At such times, there is never any shortage of paper."

❧

The fire having been lit, the improvised Italian–Ottoman co-operative had walked back to the castle, and once through the gate, had headed resolutely for the breakfast room.

They found the room all laid out, but empty. No harm done: obviously, the others had already eaten. In the Gazzolo household, Mantegazza had said, breakfast was always informal and entailed a constant coming and going; whoever woke up first ate first, and there were no assigned places. So the two men sat down on adjacent seats and rang the bell.

"Good morning, Bartolomeo," Artusi said when the butler appeared at the door. "Correct me if I'm wrong, but I seem to smell bacon and eggs. Could we have a portion?"

"I'm truly sorry, gentlemen. Right now, the kitchen is closed."

"I don't understand," said Aliyan, in a slightly resentful tone. "Are we late perhaps?"

"Absolutely not, gentlemen. This is not your fault, gentlemen." Bartolomeo coughed. "I am afraid I have some very bad news for you."

2

"Ladies and gentlemen, may I have your attention, please?"

Actually, there was no need to ask for it. Partly because Paolo Mantegazza was a magnetic orator, the kind who can impose silence with a mere glance, and partly because someone had just died, under that roof, and in such circumstances it is only natural to observe silence.

"Last night, as you all know, we lost Everardo D'Ancona, who was a friend and a faithful companion to many of us."

Mantegazza searched with his eyes for Aliyan, who stood next to Viterbo, face pale, hands trembling, lips pursed, eyes searching for something between the tiles of the floor.

"Others among us had only just started to appreciate him, to appreciate his exquisite politeness and undoubted intelligence."

Here Mantegazza shifted his gaze to Pellegrino Artusi, who stood with his hands behind his back in an attempt to hide the pomegranate stains, symbol of a festive conviviality which would have been inappropriate at such a moment.

"For this reason, before anything else, and with our host's permission, I would ask all those present to observe a minute's silence."

A tense-looking Secondo Gazzolo nodded.

Then he bowed his head, and everyone followed suit.

And everyone meant everyone. All the guests, all the servants, all the staff from the cowsheds, in short, all those who found themselves within the castle were now gathered in the large drawing room in silence, while outside the wind whistled its own funeral march for Everardo D'Ancona.

❧

"Thank you," said Mantegazza, breaking the silence after about thirty or forty seconds. "Now, again with our host's permission, I am obliged to ask you some questions."

Mantegazza's tone had changed. Now it was no longer the doctor speaking, and not even the professor. But what role he had assumed was still not clear.

"I must ask, in particular, if any of you entered Signor D'Ancona's room this morning, with or without his consent."

Silence. Different from the earlier one, however. During that silence, what had been most palpable was respect. In the almost total absence of sound right now, on the other hand, there was clearly a general feeling that respect was what had been missing from Mantegazza's question.

"Professore Mantegazza," said Signora Clara Gazzolo, her voice quivering with incredulity, "are you perhaps insinuating that one of my guests could have entered a dead man's room and stolen something?"

"I'm not insinuating anything of the sort, signora. I should only like to know if any of those present entered Signor D'Ancona's room during the night or the morning."

"I forbid you to speak to my guests in this injurious manner."

"With all due respect, Signora Clara, you have no authority to forbid me anything."

Signora Clara looked Mantegazza in the eye for a couple of seconds. Unfortunately, it is only in Victorian novels that hosts and hostesses turn their guests to stone with a look. In the Italian reality of the twentieth century, such looks are mostly harmless. Especially if the person sustaining them is someone who in his youth dodged the poisoned arrows of Amazon tribes.

Having silenced Signora Clara, Mantegazza again turned his gaze to those present.

"Gentlemen, forgive my bluntness, but I am forced to ask you this. Did any of you, for whatever reason, have access to Signor D'Ancona's room this morning?"

Silence greeted the question. A different silence again, this one more incredulous than offended. More than a silence, a ceasefire.

"So, nobody?" Mantegazza said after a few seconds.

Silence again followed. But not peace.

~ಜಿ~

"Gentlemen," Signora Clara said slyly after a few moments. "Gentlemen, I hope you are able to forgive the professor his frightful impudence. And I hope you will forgive me if I retire. I want nothing to do with this discussion."

"Clara, please stay here," said Gazzolo, kindly but firmly. "The professor isn't accusing anyone."

The signora turned to her husband with an angry look. "He isn't accusing anyone, he's accusing everyone! And of the most execrable, most horrible offence that a person could commit under the roof—"

"Are you speaking of theft, *madame*?" Mantegazza interrupted in a curt tone.

"Of course! What else?"

"I, *madame*, am speaking of murder."

~ಜಿ~

". . . That is why this morning, after I had seen Signor D'Ancona's body, I had it transferred to a room exposed to light, where I was able to carry out a summary examination . . ."

All those present listened in silence.

Everyone, without exception. The guests listened, the servants listened, and even the knights on the wall tapestries seemed to prick up their ears, anxious not to miss a single word of Paolo Mantegazza's explanation.

". . . and was thereby able to verify the presence of conjunctival petechiae, which are typically produced as a consequence of hypoxia . . ."

Secondo Gazzolo shook his head as he listened, while Corrado Viterbo didn't move a muscle but listened incredulously.

". . . a clinical picture that is consistent with the absence of cyanosis of the face, which would appear when the haemoglobin is in a reduced state . . ."

Bonci listened with narrowed eyes and his daughter with open mouth.

". . . and one that could not be of an accidental nature, insofar as an examination of the oral cavity and the oesophageal lumen did not reveal the presence of alien bodies."

And Pellegrino Artusi listened, having heard his friend talk about autopsies before, although never of a person with whom he had dined the previous evening.

"To sum up, as a result of these observations, I have been forced to conclude that Signor D'Ancona died from suffocation. He was choked to death."

～❧～

"Are you sure?" Bonci asked.

"Unfortunately, yes, my dear Signor Bonci. I have no doubt on the matter."

"But you said yourself that Signor D'Ancona suffered from a nasty disease of the respiratory tract. Couldn't he have . . . I mean, couldn't he have choked on his own . . ."

"The deceased's respiratory tract was free of mucus or other organic fluids. He died of suffocation, but there is nothing in his body that could have caused an obstruction." Mantegazza looked around. "Now, gentlemen, I hope that you will understand my question." A pause, perhaps not deliberately theatrical but theatrical all the same. "Did any of you, for whatever reason, enter Signor D'Ancona's room?"

In the silence, a hand went up.

"Yes?"

"Begging your pardon, Professore, but I have something important to say."

"Go ahead, signorina . . . I'm sorry, what's your name?"

"Crocifissa, Professore, but everyone calls me Crocetta. I'm the upstairs maid."

"Very well, Crocetta. Did you enter Signor D'Ancona's room?"

"No, I . . . I'm the upstairs maid, you see . . . and I was there this morning when I saw someone go in."

"You saw someone go in. Someone who is in this room?"

"Yes, Professore."

Said with a certain reticence, but also with a tiny desire to piss someone off, because the person in question had shown up with mud on his shoes and soiled the whole corridor just after she'd finished cleaning it.

"And at what time was this roughly?"

"It was exactly seven, sir."

Mantegazza reflected. At that hour, D'Ancona's body had already been removed from the room, even though only a few minutes earlier. "And what did this person do?"

"He knocked, he waited, he put his hand on the doorknob and went in, sir."

"Did he wait for a long time?"

"A normal time, sir. And then he went away by the stairs."

And I had to clean them again, damn him.

"And who do you think this person was?"

The maid pointed a finger towards the centre of the room. "Him, sir."

Mantegazza's eyes followed the direction of her finger, as did those of all the guests and the staff. All except Signor Reza Kemal Aliyan, on whom these eyes converged.

~~⋟⋞~~

"Signor Aliyan, I think you owe us an explanation," said Mantegazza.

Aliyan did not reply. He had turned a vermilion red, which made a striking contrast with his bright green eyes.

"Signor Aliyan, is what my maid has said true?" Gazzolo asked, taking a step or two towards the Turk. "Did you enter Signor D'Ancona's room?"

"Yes, it's true. I did go into Signor D'Ancona's room."

"And for what purpose, may I ask?"

"To get firewood."

"To do what?"

"To get firewood, Gazzolo *effendi*."

"To get firewood." Gazzolo looked at the Turk, his brows furrowed, his smile anything but pleasant. "I'm sorry, but may I ask for what purpose . . . Yes?"

Pellegrino Artusi, who had put his hand up as if he were at school, cleared his throat. "Forgive me, Signor Gazzolo, I might have something to say on the matter."

Secondo Gazzolo looked for a moment at Artusi, who was standing behind the other guests, his hand streaked with what looked like blood.

"Go ahead, my dear Signor Artusi." Gazzolo nodded, looking at that hand with a twisted smile. "Did you also kill somebody?"

"Not at all, Signor Gazzolo. In fact, what you see is the very reason Signor Aliyan went to the kitchen. This is pomegranate juice. I have it all over, as you can see." Artusi stepped forward and showed Gazzolo his shirt, which had received the decoration of the Supreme Culinary Order of the Pomegranate.

Gazzolo continued looking at Artusi, without saying a word.

"We were cooking, you see," Artusi went on. "Signor Aliyan and I were in the olive grove, where Signor Aliyan was teaching me a dish typical of his country. But we needed fire to light the outdoor stove, and we didn't have any firewood."

Artusi shot a quick glance at Gazzolo's face, to see if he was being believed or not. A pointless exercise. Gazzolo's face was like marble.

"Signor Aliyan told me he would go and get some from the kitchen, I pointed out to him that at that hour the kitchen would be topsy turvy. He might have got his clothes dirty, as I just had. So then he told me he knew where to get some. I presume he went to Signor D'Ancona's room. In fact, he returned soon afterwards, with two bundles under his arm."

"I see. So you went to Signor D'Ancona's room just to get firewood?"

"You just heard what Signor Artusi told you," Aliyan said, still red in the face.

"And why didn't you say this immediately?"

Aliyan took a deep breath before speaking. "Would you have liked to admit in public that you entered your chief's room without permission while he wasn't there?" Aliyan breathed again. "It was quite improper of me, I admit that, but nothing else. I didn't do anything wrong, I didn't think there was anything wrong."

"And you didn't take the opportunity to do anything else?" asked Mantegazza.

Aliyan looked at Mantegazza, the colour returning to his cheeks: but this time it didn't seem like embarrassment, it seemed more like anger. "I am a diplomat of the Ottoman Empire, on an official mission in your country. I am under no obligation to answer your questions."

It was no small undertaking to silence Mantegazza, but it had to be admitted that the Turk managed it to perfection. For a few seconds, at least. Then the professor quickly regained control of the situation.

"I think that at this point there is only one thing left to do." He turned to Secondo Gazzolo, who had remained stock still in front of the little group. "Secondo . . ."

Without looking at him, Gazzolo nodded briefly. Then Mantegazza embraced the whole audience with his gaze, and it was clear to everyone that the tone he was using was neither that of the doctor nor that of the academician, but rather that of senator of the Kingdom.

"Ladies and gentlemen, I think that at this point it is our duty to immediately call on the judicial authorities."

⁓

"Professore . . ."

Mantegazza was standing by the castle gate, waiting for the mail wagon, which would be passing soon, even though it was Sunday. At the beginning of the twentieth century, post offices did not close even on Christmas or New Year's Day, let alone on normal festive days.

"My dear Pellegrino, my dear Pellegrino. This is a nasty business, a truly nasty business." As Artusi approached him, Mantegazza opened his arms in a disconsolate gesture. "I confess I never thought I would find myself in a situation like this."

"I have to admit that I thought the same the first time. As you may remember, I was involved in a criminal case before."

"I remember very well," said Mantegazza.

As stated at the beginning, it certainly could not be said that the professor was someone who brought bad luck. But it might be time to raise a few doubts about Pellegrino Artusi. This was certainly not what a man of science might think, but a human being definitely would.

"Regarding that, allow me to give you a little piece of advice."

Mantegazza, still on the lookout for the mail wagon, nodded in silence, encouraging Artusi to continue.

"In the nasty affair in which I found myself some years ago" – Artusi made a gesture similar to a salute to times gone by – "the interrogations were carried out by an excellent police officer. An intelligent, upright man, who treated everyone impartially."

Mantegazza continued listening, without opening his mouth.

"You saw how Aliyan reacted to your questions. In such a delicate diplomatic situation, it may be necessary to proceed with diplomacy, but also with determination. The Turk himself will be sure to remind us of the former, but the latter will have to be provided by the investigators. As a senator of the Kingdom, do you perhaps have the power to demand that the investigation be conducted by this person?"

Without turning, Mantegazza nodded. "I can try, of course. Do you remember his name?"

"Indeed I do. Saverio Maria Artistico. I think he is now an inspector in Siena."

"Bartolomeo, I need to tell you something."

"Don't you think you've talked enough for today?"

Bartolomeo was standing by the fireplace, carefully manipulating the mechanism of the heavy chandelier, not looking at Crocetta even though she was next to him.

"I'm sorry, Bartolomeo, but the professor mentioned murder. I didn't think it was right to keep silent about what I'd seen. I thought—"

"It's not your job to think, Crocetta," Bartolomeo said as the chandelier slowly descended. "It's your job to do the rooms. Mine, right now, is to change the candles. Getting involved in the guests' private affairs isn't one of our tasks."

"All right. I understand. All the better, because what I have to tell you is also about one of the guests, and it's a private matter. In fact, very private. And I need your advice. You see . . ."

Bartolomeo raised a hand – not disdainfully, but conspiratorially. Footsteps were approaching. In fact, after a few seconds, the master of the house entered.

"Good day, Signor Gazzolo."

"Good day, sir."

"Good day to you both. What were you talking about?"

Bartolomeo carefully secured the lever before turning again and replying. The master was the master, but a chandelier that weighs a ton sometimes demands more respect. "I was advising Signorina Crocetta to be more discreet regarding the behaviour of the guests."

"Yes, it might be best, Crocetta, if next time you told me first. But that's exactly what I wanted to talk to the two of you about. Crocetta, you saw Aliyan enter Signor D'Ancona's room, is that right?"

"As God is my witness, Signor Gazzolo, I said only what I saw! And anyway, he left muddy footprints everywhere . . ."

Gazzolo turned away dismissively from the girl. "Bartolomeo, when we left the room, you locked the door with the passkey, is that right?"

"As you requested, sir."

Gazzolo nodded. He'd been sure of that anyway. It was unthinkable that Bartolomeo might forget or not carry out a request of his. It would have been more likely for the sun to rise in the west.

"And where did you put the passkey after that?"

"In its place, sir."

Gazzolo nodded again. In the third drawer of the cabinet just outside the room in which D'Ancona had slept. A place that only the master of the house and the butler knew.

"And you, Crocetta, saw Aliyan open the door just by turning the knob?"

"As God is my witness, sir."

"Are you sure?"

"Absolutely, sir."

Bartolomeo rose to his full height. His professionalism was being questioned, damn it! "I can totally assure you, sir, that I locked the door."

"Yes, yes, Bartolomeo, I don't doubt it. I remembered it, too, but I wanted to be sure. Even now, the door is locked, I checked. And the passkey is in its place. I checked just now."

Bartolomeo raised an eyebrow, even though that might have been judged indecorous. "Sir, are you saying the door was—"

"I'm saying someone opened the door and then closed it again. Someone else entered that room apart from the Turk. In fact, probably when Aliyan entered he was still inside."

Bartolomeo looked at Gazzolo and again rose to his full height. "It might be a good idea to tell the police, sir."

"Of course it's a good idea," said Crocetta. Naturally, when she'd said something like that, Bartolomeo's first thought had been to shoot her down, but now that the master was saying it, the police had to be told. Once a servant, always a servant.

Gazzolo nodded energetically. "Yes, yes. Absolutely. I'm going immediately."

3

Secondo Gazzolo shivered as he sat down at the table.

Even though Signora Clara had made sure the fire was lit, the drawing room of the castle was still cold. Of course, the room was vast, and a single fire barely sufficed even when it was full of guests. At the moment there were only two – or four, counting the polychrome wooden bishops from the Val Gardena, which contributed more than a little towards giving one the shivers, though which at least seemed appropriate to the situation.

But the main thing was that the death of a person under one's roof leaves a chill that cannot easily be overcome with a wood fire. Especially in these circumstances.

Because the other person in the room was a police officer. An inspector, to be precise. And he was there because Signor D'Ancona had not died of natural causes but had been murdered.

"Here we are, Ispettore," Gazzolo said after sitting down. "I hope this room is suitable."

"Perfectly suitable, Signor Gazzolo," Ispettore Artistico assured him, rubbing his hands on his thighs. Apart from the cold, it's perfect. Wide and high, with the dining table in a central position. That way, if we talk in low voices, we can be certain that no-one will hear us. "Indeed, I must thank you for the solicitude with which you have had everything prepared. In such situations, preparedness often turns out to be crucial in solving the case. If there is really a case to solve."

That was something the inspector had grave doubts about.

A man of almost seventy, of doubtful health and with a

touch of bronchitis to boot, who dies in his sleep without any sign of violence. If Ispettore Artistico had had to open an investigation for all the old men who kicked the bucket in their sleep, he wouldn't have had time even to go to the bathroom. Let alone take bag and baggage and leave Siena on a Sunday morning.

Unfortunately, it was not he who decided. Orders had arrived from higher up requiring his presence, having come directly from a senator of the Kingdom of which the inspector was a sincere and faithful servant. Of the Kingdom, not of the senator. In fact, if he had been able to, he would gladly have kicked the senator in that part of the body he used for sitting.

"Surely, though, there is something strange here?"

"Strange or criminal?"

"I fear the latter, though I cannot be sure. That is why I asked to speak to you now, before you interrogate all the others. I don't know if someone entered Signor D'Ancona's room while he was asleep, but what is certain is that one or more people entered it when he was already dead."

"One or more people?"

"Well, it seems to be so. This morning, after we found the body—"

"Who are 'we'?"

"Bartolomeo the butler, Mantegazza and I. We went in and found the body of poor Everardo—"

"You mean Signor D'Ancona?"

Gazzolo looked at the inspector as if wondering how many Everardos he thought died daily in the castle of Campoventoso. "Of course. We immediately saw that there was nothing that could be done, but Professore Mantegazza asked me then and there if he could examine the body in a place that was better lit. I didn't immediately understand the reason."

The inspector raised his eyebrows.

"However, I at once gave instructions for an appropriate room to be prepared and we transported the body there. Given that the door of Signor D'Ancona's room was locked, and given that he'd had with him documents of a certain importance, I thought it best to lock the door again."

"You did the right thing. And then?"

"Then, this morning, when we were gathered in this very room, it came out that one of the guests, Signor Aliyan, had entered the room after Signor D'Ancona had died."

"How did you find that out? Did he tell you?"

"No, he was seen by one of my maids."

"Who is this Signor Aliyan?"

"He's a Turkish diplomat, responsible for relations between the Ottoman Empire and the body handling the Empire's debt, a body presided over, as it happens, by Signor D'Ancona."

"So he knew him. He may have had any number of reasons to go in there."

"He may have. But I don't think the same could be said of the other man."

"What other man?"

"The one who went in before him." Gazzolo opened his hands. "I told you before that I'd had the door locked. Well, my maid swears to high heaven that she saw the man enter by simply turning the knob. Which would normally make sense. But if the door was locked—"

"Did you lock the door yourself?"

"No, not exactly. I gave orders for it to be locked."

"And who actually locked it?"

"Bartolomeo Cattoni, sir. I've been in the service of the Gazzolos since 1897."

"According to Signor Gazzolo, you were among the first to enter Signor D'Ancona's room this morning."

"That's right, sir. It was about half past six. The door was locked, so we needed my passkey."

"And who was with you?"

"Signor Gazzolo and Senator Paolo Mantegazza, who observed that the man was dead."

Senator?

"Excuse me, but are we talking about Paolo Mantegazza?"

"The very person, sir," Bartolomeo confirmed with a quarter-smile, pleased to be able to say that the castle of Campoventoso, even though no longer in the hands of a family of noble lineage, nevertheless welcomed people of a certain importance.

Ispettore Artistico also smiled.

Well, well. So the senator who had me dragged out of bed is none other than Paolo Mantegazza.

Artistico had read several of his books. Both novels and essays on medicine. The essays were very good. The novels, on the other hand, went beyond good and bad: they were terrible. This had led Ispettore Artistico to the verdict that Mantegazza must be the kind of person who never threw anything away, not even an idea.

"Did you leave the room together?"

"No, sir. Signor Gazzolo and Senator Mantegazza went to a room more appropriate for the task, while I stayed there waiting for the grooms to arrive and carry the body where requested."

"And you then locked the door again?"

"As expressly requested by Signor Gazzolo, sir."

"And the passkey you used . . ."

"It was my task to put it back in its place, sir."

"And where might this place be?"

"I don't know if it's appropriate, sir . . ."

Ispettore Artistico gave the butler a sidelong glance.

"I'm sorry, sir. The fact is that Signor Gazzolo is very particular when it comes to his guests' privacy. There is only one passkey, and I am responsible for it."

"I understand. You carry out your duties faithfully." Artistico smiled. "We all obey our superiors, Bartolomeo. I, for example, obey directly the chief inspector of Siena, who holds me responsible for the public security of his jurisdiction. A jurisdiction to which this estate and this castle also belong – you'll forgive me if I'm not able to tell you by heart the specific parcel of land. So either you tell me where you keep that damned key or I'll have you arrested."

The butler gave a slight grimace of dismay, possibly because of the threat, possibly because of the swear word, it was not clear. But it only lasted a moment. A true butler does not show his feelings in public.

"The key is in the corridor on the piano nobile, sir, in the third drawer of the cabinet beneath the tapestry depicting the battle of Cascina."

The inspector nodded, wondering how the hell he would be able to distinguish the tapestry in question. The walls of the castle, as far as he could see, were covered in tapestries, which had two things in common: one, they all depicted battles; two, they were all ugly to look at, all those figures with bobbed hair and upturned moustaches, all in profile, like ancient Egyptians in carnival fancy dress.

"And you put it back in that drawer?"

"Precisely, sir. From where I'd taken it a few minutes earlier, sir."

"Could someone have found it by chance?"

"Quite unlikely, sir. The key is carefully put back in its place.

You couldn't just find it by opening the drawer and glancing in. Especially as opening the drawer is no easy undertaking."

"I see. So whoever entered that room before Signor Aliyan, or during the night, can only have done so using that key."

"With all due respect, sir, as far as this morning is concerned, yes. But I don't think anyone can have used that key last night."

"Don't tell me it's one of your duties to sleep on top of the cabinet."

"Such an outlandish thing has never been asked of me, sir."

"You're not trying to make me believe that you were awake all night watching over the cabinet?"

A slight smile crossed the butler's face. He was sure that sooner or later he would be asked where he had been while Signor D'Ancona was being persuaded to die.

"I was indeed awake all night, sir, playing canasta with the cook and Signor Felice, the estate manager. Until five in the morning, when I went to the kitchen."

"Nobody sleeps much around here."

"The wind is getting us all a little rattled these days, sir. And these weekends are particularly busy for us servants, we're often kept up at night."

"You were telling me about that key . . ."

"Yes, sir. As I mentioned earlier, it's no easy task opening the drawer. The cabinet's old and the drawer's slightly curved, you need quite a bit of strength to open it. But that's only if the drawer hasn't been opened for some time. If the cabinet is opened and closed, for a few hours the mechanism moves much more smoothly. When I took out the key this morning, the drawer was jammed, and I had to work quite hard to shift it."

Artistico looked at the butler. "And is it moving smoothly now?"

"I haven't checked, sir. When I put back the key, it didn't give me any trouble."

"Good, then perhaps we should check it together. After which, I'll ask you to be so kind as to accompany me to Signor D'Ancona's room."

☙

"After you, sir."

Having turned the key, Bartolomeo took one step back, leaving it to the inspector to open the door, as if at his express request.

"Thank you, Bartolomeo. You may wait here."

Artistico turned the knob, went in and closed the door behind him.

A small room, not very bright, but warm. Warmer than the drawing room, but with a troublesome draught from under the door. In fact, next to the door lay one of those sausage-shaped cushions stuffed with feathers used to exclude draughts.

Artistico picked it up with two fingers.

"Bartolomeo, is this object part of the room?"

"Yes, sir. There's a bothersome draught in every room on this side."

The inspector examined it. No traces of saliva, no bites, nothing that would indicate that anyone had used the draught excluder to stifle Signor D'Ancona. Artistico dropped it back on the terracotta-tiled floor. High quality terracotta from Impruneta, as high quality as the fabric of the draught excluder.

As high quality as the faces that, a little while earlier, had witnessed the opening of the cabinet drawer from the height of their tapestry: a king and a knave, strictly in profile, whose depiction would have been more appropriate for a pack of cards than for the battle of Cascina. The drawer had been opened with some difficulty and a certain amount of noise.

"You see, sir, the last time it was opened and closed was this morning," Bartolomeo had said. "It takes a few hours for the mechanism to become slightly jammed. But if now I try to reopen it . . ."

This time, the drawer had opened easily, silently guided by the butler's gloved hand. Then, still silently, Bartolomeo had shown the inspector to the dead man's room.

Artistico stood there looking down at the floor of the room. Beautiful terracotta tiles, cleaned to perfection – apart from a few patches of mud, which went from the door to the fireplace. But not beyond. Presumably left by the Turkish diplomat. Whose name he had forgotten.

˜ఎఖ˜

"Reza Kemal Aliyan, Ispettore. I am the supervisor of the Ottoman Public Debt Administration."

Aliyan said all this making clear where the capital letters were, as if the official nature of the initials might in some way intimidate the inspector. Which was not the case.

One of the things Ispettore Artistico found hardest to tolerate was pressure, in whatever way it was applied. Whether it was official – a senator who wants you to investigate a presumed homicide – or unofficial – a bandit who informs you that your shop is made entirely of wood and could easily catch fire, unless someone takes good care of it.

Saverio Maria Artistico had been born in the hinterland of Calabria, had worked for ten years in his father's bakery, graduated in law in Naples, entered the police force in Tuscany, risen to the rank of inspector, and was now on the verge – it was said – of becoming commissioner. So he was aware of both problems.

"So you are a diplomat on a mission on behalf of your country?"

"Of our countries, Ispettore," Aliyan replied with a little smile.

The Mafia, the Camorra, or whatever name organised crime likes to give itself, is always born out of the same tacit agreement: treat your friends better than you treat everyone else. A thing we all do, some more, some less. Where, then, lay the difference between a pleasant companion and a criminal? In the codicil added by the criminals, whether they were official or unofficial: Treat your friends better than you treat everyone else, or there'll be trouble.

And what about you, Signor Aliyan? Which are you, a pleasant companion or a criminal?

"I am obliged to ask you a few questions, Signor Aliyan. A couple of them may strike you as indiscreet."

"You must do your duty, Ispettore. And my duty is to answer."

Good fellow. You got the first answer exactly right. Let's see how long that lasts, or if it's mere politeness.

"Had you known Signor D'Ancona for long?"

"For about two years. Since I joined the administration. We shared a great deal in those two years, went on many missions, signed many contracts."

"How would you describe him? What kind of person was he?"

The Turk opened his hands wide, miming an imaginary giant. "A great worker, a very honest person. Straight as a die, as you people say. And he had the memory of an elephant. Having him as a superior is – was – an honour."

"So D'Ancona was your direct superior?"

"He was the head of the governing council." Aliyan lifted his chin slightly. "One might say that I was his minister."

Alas. This Aliyan is clearly one of those people who have to make a great effort not to insert "I" into every sentence. Well, that's how we'll try to approach him.

"Let me see if I understand this. What is your role in the administration, out of curiosity?"

"I am the supervisor for the Ottoman companies who have asked for access to credit."

"I don't understand."

"If I ask you for money, *effendi*, you would lend it to me only if you were sure I could pay you back." Aliyan smiled. "I certify that the Ottoman individuals who ask for loans are in a position to pay them back."

"I see."

"And I do the same with those Italian companies that come forward to do business in Turkey, checking that they are regular, that they are sound, that they are not dealing in forbidden material."

"I see. So between you and Signor D'Ancona there was a relationship of cooperation and mutual trust?"

"I would say absolute confidence, Ispettore."

"So absolute that you would be able to enter his room in his absence?"

The Turk blushed slightly. "I can assure you that I knew nothing of—"

"Signor Aliyan, how did you come to enter that room?"

"I've already said this in front of everyone. I went in to get some firewood."

"Were you cold? You could have asked the maid."

"No, no. I wasn't cold, no. I was outside, in the olive grove, cooking."

"Cooking?"

The look on Artistico's face was obviously one of incredulity. You started well, my good fellow, but if you're starting to mess me about . . .

"One of the guests asked me to teach him a dish from my country, Ispettore, and he and I got up early this morning to prepare it together."

"And what's the name of this gentleman who wakes up at dawn in order to cook?"

"A strange name, I don't remember it exactly, something like Paladino . . ."

A circuit closed in Ispettore Artistico's head. A memory from sometime in the past, of what was definitely a real murder, and of a strange fellow, a plump, easy-going little man, dressed in an old-fashioned manner and with even more old-fashioned whiskers, but who knew the ways of the world.

"It wouldn't be Pellegrino, would it?"

"Pellegrino, yes, that's it. Pellegrino Artusi."

Ispettore Artistico shook his head, laughing. "Then everything is explained. Forgive me if I doubted you, Signor Aliyan. I know Signor Artusi personally. To learn a new dish, he'd be willing to walk to the summit of Mount Vesuvius."

The Turk opened his arms, as if he wished to embrace the room and all its contents, including the inspector. "So you believe me?"

"I believe you, Signor Aliyan."

Not because of all your jabbering and gesticulating, oh, no. Because what you're telling me matches what I've seen. There were muddy prints that went from the door to the fireplace and back. Either you took off your shoes or else you did exactly what you said. It'll be good to talk to the maid later. It'd be useful to know how much time you spent in that room.

"Then I beg you also to believe what I'm about to tell you. As I was saying, I check the reliability of those companies that wish to do business with our empire. It so happens that Signor D'Ancona and I disagreed about—"

There was a knock at the door.

"Excuse me one moment, Signor Aliyan."

Artistico walked over to the heavy oak door and opened it,

not without effort. "I asked not to be disturbed, Bartolomeo."

Standing there, Bartolomeo looked at the inspector as if he did not recognise him. "I beg your pardon, sir, but the mail wagon has arrived for the afternoon collection, and the postman needs to confer with you urgently with regard to what has happened. Signor Gazzolo asked me to admit him straight away and to inform you that he is waiting for you in the small drawing room."

And between a request from the master and one from you, Bartolomeo's expression implied, this'll show you which one matters.

"I see. One moment." The inspector went back to the centre of the room. "Signor Aliyan, I've had an urgent request. Would you be so kind as to wait for me here? As soon as I've finished, I'll be back."

❦

"Good day to you."

The postman was standing in the middle of the small drawing room, still wearing the blue cloak of his uniform. He had removed only his hat, which he held in his hand, by the peak. Nowadays, postmen can wear whatever the hell they like, but at that time postmen went around looking straight out of a catalogue of military fashion: a midnight-blue cloak, grey trousers with a red stripe and a hat with a rigid peak. The result was a hybrid, something between a dandy and a *carabiniere*, in its way not devoid of charm.

When he saw Artistico, the postman clicked his heels. "At your service, Ispettore."

What service? Alright, so you have a uniform, but that doesn't make you a soldier.

"I've been told you have something important to tell me."

"That's right, Ispettore. I heard about poor Signor D'Ancona. I knew him, he'd been coming here for a while."

The postman looked at Artistico inquisitively. He was not much more than a boy, his fashionable goatee jarring with a notable barrage of pimples. "They're saying in the village that he was murdered."

"It's possible. We're looking into that."

"Signor D'Ancona dictated a telegram to me yesterday afternoon. I think it might be important." The postman took a sheet of paper from his pocket and handed it to Artistico. "I took the liberty of bringing it."

The inspector glanced at the brief message.

Then he reread it.

"What's your name?"

"Eugenio Galgani, sir."

"You did the right thing, Galgani," said Artistico. "I'm grateful to you."

"You're welcome," replied the postman.

Artistico headed for the door, but no sooner had he placed his hand on the knob than he stopped. "I'm sorry," he said, turning. "Has the morning post already been delivered?"

The postman, who in the meantime had put his hat back on again, shook his head. "Today is Sunday, sir. The post has been collected, but not delivered."

"So it's still in the wagon?"

"Yes, sir."

Not again!

"Then if you would be so kind, I need you to hand over to me all the mail sent this morning from the castle."

The postman looked towards the door, as if suddenly discovering that he was late. "I . . . don't know if—"

"It's an order, Signor Galgani."

"I'll see to it right away, sir."

Good for you.

⸻

"So, Signor Aliyan, forgive me," said Artistico, re-entering the room. "I beg your pardon if I stay on my feet, I need to stretch my legs a little. You were starting to tell me something interesting earlier. You were telling me that you and Signor D'Ancona disagreed about something."

"That's right, Ispettore. As I was telling you, Signor D'Ancona and I almost always agreed, but sometimes frictions arose. As in this case. Based on some checking I did on a personal initiative, I had doubts about the soundness of one of the companies with which we were about to seal a deal. In fact, the agreement had already been ratified, even though I had presented a contrary opinion."

"Ah. Did you have suspicions, or did you have certainties?"

"If I had had certainties, I would have taken them to my superior. But I have reason to believe that my suspicions were well founded."

"And on whom did your suspicions fall? Can you tell me that?"

"There is no reason to hide it from you at this point. On Signor Bonci's insurance company."

"Signor Bonci. And your superior, Signor D'Ancona, didn't agree with you?"

"He said they were simply suspicions on my part, and that we could not proceed on the basis of mere suspicions."

"Right," said the inspector, nodding slowly. "Mere suspicions, of course."

He turned his back on Aliyan, took a couple of steps and

simultaneously opened the little sheet of paper that had just been brought to him.

He had read it at least four times, but now he read it again, as if afraid the words might disappear.

OPDA – CHAMBER OF COMMERCE ROME
DISCOVERED FRAUD IN PROGRESS STOP CANCEL
ALL CONTRACTS LAST SIX MONTHS STOP DETAILED
MISSIVE TO FOLLOW STOP DANCONA

4

"So, Signor Viterbo . . . May I have your first name please?"

"Corrado. Corrado Viterbo. I am a branch director of the Banca Commerciale Italiana."

"Pleased to meet you, Signor Viterbo. Do take a seat."

"I'd rather remain standing, if you don't mind."

I believe you. Signor Corrado Viterbo had the name of a city and a waistline the size of a province. The small chair with arms, in front of the table, would have been an instrument of torture for him.

"This might be a long interview. If you prefer, we could make ourselves comfortable in the armchairs."

"That's very kind of you," Viterbo said, refusing with a gesture of his right hand. "But I'm a little shaken, and I wouldn't be able to stay seated, believe me."

"Did you know Signor D'Ancona well?"

"Yes, we'd known each other for some time. When he was appointed to direct the OPDA, I was introduced to him by our host, Signor Gazzolo. I had already worked with him – with Gazzolo, I mean – previously."

"So he brought you in on Gazzolo's recommendation?"

Signor Viterbo shook his head. "I doubt that. He will have gathered his own information. Everardo was a cautious man."

Indeed.

From the little Ispettore Artistico had found out so far about Everardo D'Ancona, if he had had to choose an adjective to describe him, he would no doubt have chosen that one.

Cautious.

How else could you define someone who sent important messages by carrier pigeon?

～╲╱〜

"Signor D'Ancona was a gentleman of the old school, and he trusted completely in my abilities," Bartolomeo had said as they climbed the stairs that led to the pigeon loft.

A mere hour earlier, after discovering the telegram, Ispettore Artistico had immediately done what he could to intercept the letter that the telegram itself announced: the detailed missive in which D'Ancona had apparently described the fraud he had discovered.

He had ordered the postman to hand over all the mail collected from the castle that morning.

But then Signor Aliyan had told him that Signor D'Ancona would never have sent such an important message by ordinary mail.

～╲╱〜

"Pigeons are faster and safer. A letter takes two days to get to Rome by post, a pigeon takes four hours. We're in the country here, not in Milan or Rome." Aliyan had made a gesture as if scrunching something. "Besides, a letter can be intercepted. Anyone can pay the postman. But who can intercept a pigeon?"

"Someone who's a good shot."

"You're joking, but I'm serious. Signor D'Ancona can only have sent that letter by pigeon. If he was able to do so in time."

And so the inspector had climbed into the pigeon loft together with Bartolomeo, who dealt personally with those pigeons still able to fly, in addition to serving those that had been roasted.

"Here we are," the butler had said once they arrived in the pigeon loft, a well-lit but filthy space to which the only access was via a stepladder. "Look. Those with the red bands are for Rome, those with the black bands for Milan. But I couldn't swear to it, it might be the opposite."

"Isn't it up to you to send the messages, Bartolomeo?"

"No, Signor D'Ancona saw to that personally."

The inspector had looked back down the stepladder and wondered how an old man with a touch of emphysema could have climbed up that thing. Then he looked at the pigeons and concluded that he had obviously not done so this time. There were still four pigeons.

⋅⋇⋅

"And what kinds of transactions were you dealing with during this weekend?" the inspector asked Signor Viterbo.

"I can't go into the details of the operations. These are private matters."

Signor Viterbo smiled.

This is not a postman eager to make himself useful, this is a kind of shark. Careful, Saverio. Best to keep your distance. Well, that shouldn't be too hard with this fellow. But what is all this nonsense I'm thinking? All right, Saverio, if he's a shark, act like a shark. Circle him.

"For now, all I need to know are the individuals involved and what they were negotiating."

"That's no secret. There are three individuals in play: Signor Gazzolo for the provision of foodstuffs to the army, Signor Bonci for the provision of insurance services to the officers of the Ottoman Empire, and Signor Artusi for the purchase of valuable textiles."

"Are these negotiations at an advanced stage?"

"Signor Gazzolo's is ongoing. We've been doing business with the Ottomans for two years now, and new pieces of the mosaic are constantly being added. Signor Bonci's still has to be finalised, but as there had already been a previous contract with his company, only a few details needed to be filled in. Signor Artusi's is only just starting."

"How do these negotiations work? Or rather, how do they conclude?"

"They conclude with an official licence issued by the OPDA, which authorises the licensee to trade with the Sublime Porte."

"And who signs these licences?"

"Signor Everardo D'Ancona together with Vizir Haroun al-Sulayman."

"And is it impossible to trade with the empire without such a licence?"

"To even try would be considered a crime. Both by Italy and above all by the Ottomans."

Ispettore Artistico, who had also remained standing, began to walk in a fairly broad circle around Viterbo. "So such a licence has an intrinsic value."

Signor Viterbo laughed heartily. "Definitely. It's a passport to a market of thirty million people."

"Could you describe it to me?"

"It's a kind of papyrus in a frame embellished with geometric patterns. The text is in Arabic and Italian and says—"

"Could you by any chance show me one?"

"Only Signor D'Ancona had them. The one intended for Signor Bonci should be in his room."

"Yes. It should be. A pity that it isn't."

"It isn't there? Impossible. It was due to be handed over to him today."

"I'm pleased for him. But it's not there."

Having walked a full circle, Artistico went and placed himself in front of Viterbo, his hands on his hips. "A little while ago, I went with Signor Aliyan to D'Ancona's room, to look through his papers. We went through them one by one. That document isn't there."

"But it should have been."

"That's what Signor Aliyan says, too."

"Couldn't Signor Aliyan have taken it?"

"Not in my presence. I was there personally going through the papers, taking them one by one and showing them to him. I didn't notice any document similar to the one you described to me. And which Aliyan has described in an identical way."

"Didn't you trust Aliyan?"

"I don't trust anyone, Signor Viterbo, when I'm working on a case. I don't trust Aliyan, I don't trust you, and I don't trust Signor Bonci."

Although the latter seems to me deserving of particular attention.

"Do you know Signor Bonci well?"

"We've known each other for about a year."

Said with a slight hesitation, as if he were confessing something.

"Always and only in connection with business?"

"Yes, yes."

Two yeses, when one would have been enough?

"Are you sure?"

"It's something that has nothing to do with what we're talking about."

"I'd rather be the one to ascertain that, if you don't mind."

"The thing is, Signor Bonci has a daughter. Delia. A dear creature."

"I understand," Artistico replied, delicately. "How old is your son?"

Viterbo let his eyes wander halfway around the room, just so as not to look at the inspector. "Oh, no, Ispettore. I don't have any children."

I don't believe it. This obese old man is in love with Bonci's daughter.

"And you intended . . ."

"If this . . . this horrible thing hadn't happened, I would have asked Signor Bonci for his daughter's hand this very day, yes." Viterbo took a big fat breath, as big and fat as he was. "I've been a widower for years, I never had children. And I'm alone. Delia, Signorina Bonci, came to me every Wednesday, on her father's behalf, with the documents and files I needed to analyse his company's finances."

This time, Viterbo looked at the inspector. Two big eyes, like a child's, with large pupils and resigned eyebrows.

"What can I tell you, Ispettore? I found myself waiting for three o'clock on Wednesday afternoon as if it were the most important appointment of the week."

"And wasn't it?"

Shrugging, the banker took his eyes away from the inspector. "From a strictly financial point of view, no. The finances were of no great interest, but easy to deal with."

"What did you examine in your analysis?"

"It's an insurance company, so I looked at the number of clients, the demands of collection, the punctuality of premium payments, the possibility of accidents . . ."

"And you say the finances were satisfactory?"

Viterbo looked again at the inspector. This time, however, there was nothing tender in his gaze. "May I know why you are asking these questions about Signor Bonci's finances?"

"I'm sorry, that's confidential information."

"In other words, you're telling me that Bonci is in trouble."

"I'm not telling you anything at all," said Artistico, looking straight between Viterbo's eyebrows.

When I'm on a case, I don't trust anyone or anything, that look said.

Whereas it seems to me I've been a bit too trusting, Signor Viterbo's look clearly responded.

❦

"I think you have to tell him."

"Do you really think so? I don't know. I'm not sure."

"Please don't be upset, Professore, but I'd like to understand what exactly it is you're not sure of. What you saw, or what you should do."

"Oh, my dear Pellegrino . . ." Mantegazza rubbed the side of his nose, next to the nostril, a gesture typical of a polite person resisting the temptation to pick his nose in public. "I have to be honest. It's the latter. You do understand what the consequences would be if I did it?"

"Of course. Of course. But I ask you: what would the consequences be if you didn't do it?"

Mantegazza nodded very slowly, passing his index finger over his throat. "Yes. Yes."

❦

"May I?"

"Come in, come in, signorina."

The girl raised her eyebrows, almost surprised. "Signorina? Me? I'm sorry, I'm not used to it."

"All right, then. What are you used to?"

"Actually, everybody calls me Crocetta."

"Is that your name? Please, sit down."

The girl looked around circumspectly, then sat down. Not on the edge of the stool, but solidly in the middle. The policeman had said "sit down", and she had sat down.

"I'll spare you my full name or you'll start laughing, and with a dead body in the house that wouldn't be right."

The inspector smiled. "Alright, Crocetta. So, I'm told that it was you who saw Signor Aliyan go into Signor D'Ancona's room this morning. Is that right?"

"Yes, it is. If I said it, that means I saw him."

"And how did he go in? Did he use a key?"

"No, he knocked, he waited and he went in."

"And what did you do?"

Crocetta pulled an incredulous face. She was odd-looking: not beautiful, certainly not, but unusual, friendly. Round eyes, a broad nose, very white teeth. She looked like a kind of mischievous frog.

"Well, I just stayed there like an idiot with my rag in my hand, waiting for him to bugger off so I could carry on cleaning. He left a streak like a snail."

"I see. I assume you had to wait a long time."

This was asked casually, as if it were not a question but an observation of pure empathy. Actually, it was the crucial question, the one he had summoned her for.

Couldn't Aliyan have stolen it? Of course, dear Signor Viterbo. Do you think I hadn't already thought of that? You're not going to teach your grandmother to suck eggs, are you? But to have stolen the document, he will have needed a modicum of time.

Crocetta shook her head. "No, he came out right away. Not even half an Ave Maria."

"Do you measure time in prayers?"

"No, but I'd just started one to ask forgiveness of the Virgin Mary for all the things I'd wished on him."

"And when he came out, was he holding anything in his hand?"

"I couldn't say, sir. I was looking at his shoes. There was a kilo of mud on them. If he'd walked on the carpet, he wouldn't need an Ave Maria, he'd need a De profundis. Sorry, I didn't mean to say that."

"Don't worry, Crocetta. It doesn't matter how you tell me things, what matters is what you tell me."

"I wish they were all like you. Because as it happens, there's something else I could tell you."

"Also about Aliyan?"

"Oh, yes. You see, the gentleman's sort of in the habit of going into other people's rooms."

The inspector's face clouded over. "That's a serious accusation, Crocetta."

"Accusation? Oh, no, sir. I don't think you understand. This Turk with his fair hair and green eyes did go into someone else's room, but with their permission." She gave Artistico a fox-like look. "You see, I'm an upstairs maid, which means I do the rooms. The rooms and the beds. And two people slept in Signorina Delia's bed last night. Not that they did much sleeping, if you ask me."

"But you can't know it was Aliyan," replied Artistico, incredulous, trying to dismiss from his mind the horrible image of a naked Signor Viterbo throwing himself on poor Delia.

Crocetta nodded vigorously. "Trust me. Apart from the fact that he raised hell to get his room changed. This one's too far to the north, that's one's too far to the south, this one's dark. In the end he argued so much, he managed to get a room next to Signorina Delia's. It may be coincidence. But Signorina Delia's bed definitely smelled of roses this morning. Roses and musk. The very same perfume as Signor Aliyan's."

"You can't be certain. It's a common essence."

Crocetta looked at the inspector with a hint of resentment. "You're telling me I can't be certain? You use a scent called Fougère Royale, don't you?"

This time it was Artistico who looked at Crocetta as if she had just given him a slap.

His wife's twentieth wedding anniversary present to him. The only one he had ever used – Ispettore Artistico hated perfumes but loved his wife. A French eau de cologne with a name you couldn't pronounce – at least he couldn't.

But that was the one, without doubt. Fougère Royale by Houbigant.

Crocetta nodded. "You have it on right now. It smells good, it smells of newly mown grass. And bergamot. It was used by a guest of Signor Gazzolo's, Signor Pizzi. I could tell you what cologne all the guests here use, and I wouldn't make a single mistake, trust me."

5

"Please take a seat, Professore. I'm sorry to have kept you waiting, but I preferred to start by questioning the people most directly involved."

"No problem, no problem," Mantegazza said, sitting down and pouring himself a generous dose of water from the carafe on the table.

Ispettore Artistico, his hands joined, waited for the professor, who seemed more nervous than thirsty, to take a sip from the glass. Then he began speaking.

"I won't hide from you the fact that, given your fame, I considered it unproductive for the investigation to begin with your point of view on the matter. You have already given your verdict – you believe that Signor D'Ancona died a violent death – and I'm sure you have valid reasons for doing so."

And besides, even just talking with the master of the house, I've discovered another seven or eight crimes, some that violated the penal code, others common morality, so any presumed homicide went straight out of my head.

"Oh, yes."

Was that all? He might have been expected Professore Mantegazza, a senator of the Kingdom, to be much more self-confident. He was acting almost liked a schoolboy called to the blackboard.

"But, as I'm sure you'll understand, as a policeman I have to ask you to repeat the reasons why you consider this to have been a criminal act."

Mantegazza, who had taken a further sip of his drink, nodded and appeared to regain strength. "Yes, there can be no doubt about it. Poor Signor D'Ancona died after being suffocated by an external agent. The presence of conjunctival petechiae was the first thing that made me suspect it. The pitch-black colour of the blood and the—"

"I'm sorry to interrupt you, Professore. You're telling me that Signor D'Ancona died of asphyxia, but not that this asphyxia was of a violent nature. Couldn't it have come about as a complication of his illness? I've been told that Signor D'Ancona had a touch of bronchitis."

"No, not at all. Such a complication would have caused hypoxaemic respiratory failure, in other words, respiratory failure due to lack of oxygen. The air goes in, but the oxygen is not replaced by the lung tissue. But in that case the patient's skin should have been cyanotic, bluish, and it wasn't. That means that the respiratory failure was of a hypercapnic type, in other words, due to an excessive accumulation of carbon dioxide, which typically only occurs when the airways are obstructed." Here, rather appropriately, Mantegazza took a deep breath. "Which brings us to our problem."

"That, according to you, someone deliberately suffocated Signor D'Ancona?"

"Yes, that's precisely the point. You see, Signor D'Ancona was suffering from bronchitis, which is why I advised him not to light the fire in his room. But the room in which he was staying clearly had a tiresome draught coming in from under the door."

"Yes, of course. I saw one of those stuffed draught excluders by the door."

"There you are. When I entered the room this morning . . . I was the first to enter, did you know that?"

"Yes, so I was told."

"Well, when I went in, I immediately felt that the door was resisting somewhat. That was because of the draught excluder, which had been pushed rather carefully under the crack. At the time, I didn't take any notice, I was more concerned with Signor D'Ancona's health. But thinking back on it . . ."

But thinking back on it.

"If the draught excluder was there, it means the door had been closed from the inside. And so nobody could have gone in during the night. Is that what you're saying?"

"Actually, yes."

"And so?"

"And so, if nobody can have entered from outside, nobody can have suffocated Signor D'Ancona."

And so, I made you come here for nothing, said the professor's eyes, not without embarrassment.

For a moment, the inspector drummed his fingers on the desk.

Bartolomeo had said that nobody took the key during the night. Now Mantegazza was confirming that the room had remained locked all night long. Therefore nobody had entered the room.

Which didn't mean that nobody had taken poor Signor D'Ancona's life. Because motives for his death had emerged, rather a lot of them, in fact.

Arriving at the castle, Ispettore Artistico had been convinced he would be obliged to take into account the words of a senator eager for attention, but no more than that. His opinion had changed. Something had happened here.

It was clear that D'Ancona had discovered something wrong in a business deal – the one involving Bonci seemed the likeliest. It was equally clear that somebody had stolen a licence authorising trade with the Ottoman Empire – and this time it was almost certainly Bonci's.

Where do two lines meet? In a point, Saverio.

◦◦◦

"Excuse me, Professore. Earlier, you said 'typically by obstruction of the airways'. What does that mean?"

"That suffocation occurs when a person cannot inhale enough air."

"And is obstruction of the airways the only way to obtain this result?"

"Oh, no. For example, and this is just an example, if a person blocks the individual's ribcage in such a way as to prevent its expansion . . ."

The inspector waved his hand. "I wasn't thinking of such a complicated expedient. Those things happen only in detective stories. No, what I was wondering was: what if somebody drugged the wine or the drink of a person who has a serious lung disorder, using a powerful sleeping draught?"

Slowly, the professor's face lit up, and he looked straight at the inspector as if only now recognising him as a fellow creature. "Oh, God, it could be, you know. It could be. Relaxation induced by sedation can certainly lead to suffocation. The native peoples of the Amazon use arrows poisoned with similar substances, and death occurs through paralysis of the respiratory muscle. Waterton demonstrated that as long ago as 1820. He took a mule and—"

Like Ispettore Artistico cared a jot about Waterton. "And would there be traces of these substances in the blood?"

"Traces? In order to sedate a man to the point of suffocation, you would have to give him a barrelful of these substances. But it would be more sensible to look in the stomach and the innards.

Curare, for example, acts if it enters the bloodstream, although very little of what is ingested gets into the blood. Most remains in the digestive tract."

"So a laboratory of chemical analysis could identify them?"

"Certainly."

"I see. Could you collect some samples from the corpse, and then suggest a laboratory I can trust?"

❧

"Please sit down, Signor Bonci. By the way, what's your Christian name?"

Signor Bonci sat down and peered around with suspicious little eyes. Then, supporting himself with his hands on his thighs, he leaned towards the inspector and looked him straight in the face.

"Seeing that you are finally taking the trouble to question me, I shall tell you. My name is Giuseppe Bonci, and I was born in Pisa on the tenth of June 1850."

Clearly a nice person, this Signor Bonci.

"I'm sorry you have the impression that you've been neglected. You know, in these cases it is only fitting to question those present one at a time. There are always some who are questioned first, and some last."

Bonci shook his head, like someone who is always having to deal with other people's ignorance. "Perhaps so, but if you had questioned me first you might have spared yourself a great deal of effort." Bonci gave a pig-like little smile. "However, what's done is done. So, correct me if I'm mistaken: Signor D'Ancona, may he rest in peace, was suffocated in his own room, a room that was locked and to which there was no way of gaining access, is that right?"

"Let me correct you immediately, Signor Bonci: I'm the one who asks the questions here. You may have the courtesy to answer or to keep silent, in which case you assume the responsibility."

Bonci looked at Artistico in surprise. "Indeed, Ispettore. You've come here from Siena, haven't you? Is your direct superior by any chance Ispettore Bianco, of Pisa?"

Of all the moves that Signor Giuseppe Bonci could have made, this was absolutely the most mistaken of all.

"I see you still don't understand whose job it is to ask the questions here. Do you realise that you are within a hair's breadth of making yourself liable to arrest for insulting a public official?"

Bonci stiffened like a wooden statue, the kind he liked so much.

In order to do business with the Ottoman Empire, one of the conditions set by the Chamber of Commerce was that the proponents should be persons of pristine honesty, at least officially. In fact, whereas in dealing with the Ottoman Empire the other European countries sent the representatives of banks and government agents, the Italians had sent a much vaster and more heterogeneous group. It is not the banks who do business with you, said Italy to the empire on the Bosphorus, it is the Italian people, it is the whole of Italy.

But the larger the group, the easier it is to find criminals among them. That was why Signor D'Ancona had been clear: a clean criminal record. Any previous conviction or any trouble with the law, and the deal would be strangled at birth. We don't want them to think they are dealing with people who could screw them, we want to screw them and even be thanked for it.

Getting arrested would set an inexorable mechanism in motion: the OPDA, having received notification of the offence from the police would inform the Chamber of Commerce, which would take Signor Bonci and kick him from here to eternity.

"I just wanted to be of help, Ispettore."

"You will be of much more help if you let me do my job. However, if you feel more comfortable making a statement of your own free will before I question you, perhaps now is the time to do so."

"Well, Ispettore, we're in an old castle, one that dates back to 1350. As I'm sure you know, these castles often had secret passages, tunnels that led all the way outside, so that the lord of the manor could escape if need be. If you had to build such a passage, where would you start it from?"

"From the lord's bedroom."

"Of course. And the lord's bedroom, the largest bedroom in the castle, was originally the one in which Signor D'Ancona slept. Only, a few years ago Signor Gazzolo had it divided into two smaller rooms, in order to be able to heat them better."

"And you're saying that this castle has a passage like that?"

"On the east side of the castle, there's a secret door, which opens in a particular way and leads somewhere."

Ispettore Artistico shook his head dubiously. "Signor Gazzolo didn't say anything to me about it."

"I'm sure he wouldn't be pleased if anyone investigated that tunnel. There must be something quite dangerous in it, if Gazzolo puts on a fencing mask when he goes in."

"A fencing mask? Have you seen that with your own eyes?"

"Yes, or rather, no. My daughter told me."

"Your daughter told you."

Signor Bonci looked at the inspector. Only two people repeated your last words like that, as if weighing them up: one of them was Professore Mantegazza, and the other . . .

"Don't you believe me?"

Of course he did. A secret passage leading to the most remote rooms of the castle, through which hordes of assassins thirsty for blood can enter. Maybe your daughter reads a few too many gothic novels.

"I don't believe anything or anyone until I can verify it for myself, Signor Bonci. I think now would be a good time for me to speak to your daughter."

~∗~

At that moment, Delia Bonci was moving around outside the castle, along the north wall. It was cold here, there was wind and mud, but Papa wasn't here. Which meant that, from Delia Bonci's point of view, the positives outweighed the negatives.

As she walked, she was thinking.

Reaching the north-east corner, she turned it, walked another fifty paces, then stopped.

There in front of her was the door. It was quite visible from close up. A rectangle of bricks without any mortar around it, forming a serrated outline, practically impossible to see from the outside, but from this distance it stood out.

But what could be in there? A dangerous animal?

A tiger? Unlikely.

Bees, perhaps?

Bees that sting the slothful, just like in the Divine Comedy. And what was she? Certainly not a sloth. She had made her mind up; she had done something.

Let's hope that nobody saw me.

Steps could be heard behind the door. Delia looked around. Next to the door were two large hedges, nothing else.

Now how can I make sure I'm not seen?

~∗~

In the darkness Crocetta moved silently, taking care not to bump into anything. And in the meantime, she was pondering.

Of all the plants in the world, those two had to cook with pomegranates, Crocetta thought as she proceeded cautiously along the tunnel, her mask pulled well down over her head. They soiled all my towels for me. Now I have to work my socks off getting them clean. Damn them and their obsessions. Bartolomeo's right, they can't even wait to be served, they have to do things for themselves.

And this place. A tunnel, they call it. It's just a sewer, that's all it is. I suppose *tunnel* sounds English, and they're obsessed with using English words. Of course, it might be nice to learn English. But what use would that be to you, Crocetta? You're going to spend your whole life stuck here in Campoventoso.

With her hands, in the dark, Crocetta found what she was looking for. She sniffed it, it was fine.

Right, let's go back.

~☙~

The footsteps were very close. Delia instinctively crouched behind one of the two hedges next to the door. An osmanthus hedge, with small, fragrant flowers.

The door opened and a young woman came out, wearing a white apron and with sandals on her feet.

And a fencing mask on her face. Delia closed her eyes and held her breath.

~☙~

"Had you known Signor D'Ancona for a long time?"

"For about a year. Ever since I proposed my company as a

liaison with the Ottoman Empire. For about a year now, I've been going back and forth between Turkey and Italy."

"Were you good friends?"

"We had a business relationship, but a mutually respectful one. Each was essential to the other."

"And did you know any of the other weekend guests before coming here?"

"Signor Viterbo and I have seen a lot of each other. He's a good person."

"Have you seen each other purely on a business footing?"

Signor Bonci gave a broad smile and made a vague gesture with his hand. "My daughter and Signor Viterbo get along very well. You're an experienced man, I don't think there's any need to add anything else."

Ispettore Artistico nodded pensively. "I see. And what about the others, what can you tell me about them?"

"Secondo Gazzolo and I have known each other for some time, he is also my client. As for the others, what can I tell you, Ispettore? I am a man of quite another ilk, like you."

What do you know about it?

"When I listen to the arguments of unbelievers, I feel the blood go to my head. I'm not saying that this Professore Mantegazza isn't a great luminary, but he's the kind of person who's convinced he knows everything. The kind who thinks the Almighty doesn't hear them when they boast about monkeys turning into men, or men and pigs fighting over food."

Ispettore Artistico let his eyes wander towards the far end of the room and come to rest on the two bishops, who silently approved, polychrome but unanimous.

"And what about Signor Aliyan?"

"Signor Aliyan is full of hot air. He thinks he's the head of the Ottoman Empire, but he's only a mediocre pen pusher."

As cut and dried as that.

"Do you know him well?"

"As much as I need to. Our relations are purely administrative. For the rest, Ispettore, and I make no bones about this, the less I see him the better."

❦

Calmly, Crocetta whistled, carrying the bundle under her arm inside the fencing mask, like a basket. After closing the door, she had put the peg back in its place, without noticing anything unusual, and had headed for the entrance gate. These escapes from the castle, taking three times longer to go anywhere than was strictly necessary, were one of the favourite moments of her day.

After all, who's going to notice me?

Now I have to make an effort. Do everything by myself, as usual. And do it invisibly, as usual. Or rather, not as usual. If you do your job well, nobody notices you. If you do it badly, everyone gets at you.

❦

Delia started to breathe again only when she saw the woman turn the corner of the castle wall. The scent of the osmanthus flowers entered her nose like a liberation.

After a few seconds, she came out from behind the hedge and looked at it again.

Thank you, hedge. Thank you for protecting me with the embrace of your leaves.

You were my ideal accomplice, hedge. Flowery, fragrant and beautiful to look at.

You're what they would like me to become. A plant.

Signor Bonci stood up, making a noise with his chair, and adjusted his jacket.

"If you'll allow me, Ispettore, I would like to ask you a question after all. Why on earth did you keep me for last?"

Because you're the prime suspect, my friend. But I'm not going to tell you that. And besides . . .

"You're not the last, Signor Bonci. Before anything else, I need to speak as soon as possible with your daughter."

Alright, said Bonci's eyes. I was speaking about people, not women.

"After which, there's still one more person I'd like to question."

"Oh yes, the cookery fellow. You can have him, as far as I'm concerned. In my opinion he's nothing but a socialist."

The square root of 32

"Please sit down, signorina."

Delia sat down, shifting her skirt to one side, almost in the Amazon style. But the resemblance ended there. Eyes down, knees tight together, hands in her lap, there was much more defence than attack in the posture of Signor Bonci's daughter.

"Now then, signorina, I need to ask you some questions. Some of these questions are personal, so I ask you to forgive me if I seem impudent."

The young woman nodded, without speaking.

"To start with, I wanted to know if it's true that you saw a concealed passage within the walls of the castle."

"Did Papa tell you that?"

"Yes, it was your father who told me."

"Yes, it's true." Delia nodded, energetically. "There is a door on the side where the sun sets. It's opened with a kind of peg, and it's really quite disturbing."

"Did you see someone go in?"

"Yes. Two people. Or rather, one went in and the other came out. Two people who . . . well, it's strange. They were both wearing masks, the kind, you know that are used—"

"In fencing?"

"Yes, that's right."

"Who did you see go in?

"Signor Gazzolo. It was on Saturday. Today, a little while ago, I saw a woman come out. I think it was one of the maids, I may have seen her around the castle in the last few days. She certainly isn't one of us."

"What do you mean by that?"

"I mean she isn't one of the guests. I know all of them by now, and besides, I'm the only woman among them."

"What did they do?"

"I don't know. Signor Gazzolo went in. The woman, the maid, came out. That's all I saw."

"Do you have any idea what might be in there?"

Delia looked straight at the inspector with eyes as large as her doubts.

How should I know? Bees? Stinging plants? The Minotaur?

Maybe there's a labyrinth under the castle, and I'll end up like Ariadne, seduced and abandoned, lost in the intricacies of a kind of fairy tale I've constructed around myself, with the handsome prince arriving from far away and promising to take me away but then leaving and I'm stuck here, praying my belly doesn't get big.

Ispettore Artistico nodded. All right, the story of the door was true, but who could tell what was behind it? Now that the young woman seemed more malleable, it was time to probe a little deeper.

"Are you acquainted with any of the weekend guests?"

"Some, not all."

"Who, for example?"

"Signor Viterbo and Papa have known each other for a while."

"What about Signor Aliyan?"

"I couldn't say. He and Papa don't get on well."

I asked you who you are acquainted with, signorina, not who your father knows, Ispettore Artistico would have liked to scream. But it would have been pointless. The girl had closed up like a clam. He would have to put the knife in gently, not hack and slash away.

"You said Signor Viterbo is a friend of your father's. He seems like a good person."

Delia looked down at her hands, which lay in her lap. The knuckles were white. "A very good person, yes."

"I imagine he's also a friend of the family. Have you been seeing him for a long time?"

"For about a year."

"And do you intend to keep seeing him in the future?"

Delia again looked up at the inspector. Her eyes were filled with tears.

"So you know?"

~~~

"May I?"

"Ah, my dear Signor Artusi, please come in."

"My dear Ispettore, tragic as the circumstances are, it's a real pleasure to see you again."

"As it is for me, Signor Artusi. I see you're in great form."

It was true. Steady eyes, a firm gait, no stick or glasses or any other of the proprioceptive aids that were the norm for the over-seventies at the beginning of the last century. And he still had those whiskers in the style of an Austro–Hungarian lieutenant, nicely curled and groomed.

"The years are passing, Ispettore. An entire lustrum in our case."

I didn't think I would ever again hear anyone use the word "lustrum" in a conversation in my lifetime. A man from another age, was dear old Pellegrino. But at last a man. Not a shifty gnome like Bonci or a scared young girl like Delia. Someone with whom one could talk freely.

"I hope it's pure chance, my dear Signor Artusi, that we meet again over a criminal matter. If I were superstitious, as people are in my part of the world, I would have to arrest you. You are always at the scene of the crime."

Earlier, to two different people, Ispettore Artistico had said that he couldn't trust anybody. There was, however, one exception: the man who now stood in front of him, who years earlier had shown his trust in him and had been an extremely valuable witness, crucial to the solution of a case. The first murder Saverio Maria Artistico had ever investigated, the moment his career in the police had really taken off. From the unhealthy marshes of the Maremma to the palaces of Siena, where he had arrived freshly promoted. Where his wife had stopped complaining, where his daughter would go on to marry the scion of one of the richest families in the city.

All things which, it had to be honestly admitted, would never have happened without Signor Pellegrino Artusi from Forlimpopoli.

Such things cannot be forgotten.

Artusi smiled beneath his snow-white vegetation, then sat down, slowly shaking his head. "So it really was a murder?"

"Everything seems to indicate it, yes. I can't say more than that. But you might perhaps be able to help me."

"I am at your disposal, Ispettore."

"Could you tell me how last night's dinner went?"

Artusi raised his eyebrows. "Gladly – what I can remember, that is. What exactly do you want to know?"

"Before anything else, let's start with the things you remember clearly. What did you eat at dinner?"

Artusi smiled. "That certainly doesn't require poor Signor D'Ancona's prodigious memory. They were all dishes I know very well." He continued to smile, his eyes growing very small above his very large whiskers. "The hostess, Signora Clara, tried to honour me by serving dishes taken from my own treatise."

"You'll have to get used to that, Signor Artusi. You're famous now."

"More than I thought. Even Signor D'Ancona told me he had read my book. At the time, I thought he was only saying that out of politeness, but when head of lamb was served, I told an amusing little story. I said I was pleased that the head had been cut lengthwise, and not across, as a serving maid of my acquaintance had done: the same girl who had once skewered thrushes on the spit the wrong way round. It's the same story I tell in my little manual, before the recipe for head of lamb. Signor D'Ancona laughed and said that the stories in my book were always highly entertaining, and that Recipe no. 176 would have been more appropriate for that evening. That means he had recognised the story and knew that it appeared in my book."

Good heavens. A genuinely prodigious memory, Signor D'Ancona's.

"And what is the story of number 176?"

Artusi opened his arms wide. If he remembered correctly, that was the recipe for fried artichokes. The kind they only know how to make in Tuscany, because in other places they either boil them first or put them in batter. D'Ancona's intention had probably been to compliment the hostess's fried dish. But with all those new editions, even Artusi may have got confused.

"Alas, Signor D'Ancona remembered my book much better than I. I gave him a worldly smile and changed the subject. As I've just done, for which I apologise. You asked me what we had for dinner." Artusi started counting on his fingers. "So, as a starter, figs with ham and salted anchovies. As a fried course, small rolls filled with sweetbreads. As an intermediate course, a mushroom flan with chicken giblets."

For Artistico, that would have sufficed for dinner. From the way in which Artusi had begun to list the courses, it was obvious that Signora Clara's guests hadn't even got halfway.

"As stew, duck with egg pasta from Arezzo, and the head of lamb that I already mentioned. As roast, beef roasted on the spit with potatoes."

And they say we Calabrians are big eaters!

"Anything else?"

"No, the roast beef was the last dish."

Thank God for that.

"From there, we went straight on to the dessert."

Oh, of course. I was starting to wonder.

"An apricot jam *crostata*, very nicely baked as it happens, and a pudding of toasted almonds."

"And then how did the evening continue?"

"It didn't. The dinner was long and pleasant, but since there had been some little quarrels over lunch, we were not inclined to linger."

"I see. Given those disagreements, did the table arrangements cause any problems?"

"No, Signora Clara is too shrewd, and the butler is a walking book of etiquette. Have you met him?"

"Bartolomeo? He strikes me as someone who would die on the ramparts for his own family. Signor and Signora Gazzolo, that is."

Artusi laughed. "Indeed he would. Anyway, the places had been somewhat redistributed. I was seated between Signora Clara and Signor Aliyan. On the other side of the signora was Signor D'Ancona, then next to him Signor Bonci, with his daughter by his side, as usual. To the left of Signorina Delia was Signor Viterbo . . ."

The inspector shuddered.

". . . and to the left of Viterbo were Signor Gazzolo and Professore Mantegazza. Yes, that's how it was."

"So Bonci was next to D'Ancona?"

"Precisely."

"Let's see if I've got this right." The inspector made a circle on the table with his index finger and started to surround it with finger marks. "Bonci was next to D'Ancona, and Signor Aliyan was on the other side. I seem to have gathered that it was between those two that the disagreements had arisen."

"Yes, that's right."

"Do you know the reason for these disagreements?"

How can I be unaware of it? The Turk must surely know that the love of his life has been promised in marriage to a banker who's twice his age and weighs three times what he does. I don't know if Bonci knows that the Turk has had his hands all over his daughter. It seems to me he'll have to find out sooner or later.

"Some of the guests told me there were a number of petty remarks about religion," the inspector said, prompting him, but Artusi shook his head.

"Which in my opinion don't matter a fig to either of them. You see, Ispettore, I talked with Signor Aliyan this morning."

"While the two of you were cooking?"

"Precisely. I can tell you what he said, though I should point out that I heard only his point of view."

"Go ahead."

"Signor Aliyan suspected that Bonci was committing some kind of fraud. He said that Bonci had presented an impressive series of documents and policies testifying to the size and health of his business. You know he's an insurance agent, don't you?"

The inspector nodded, in silence.

"Well, Aliyan has a suspicion, or rather, according to him, the certainty that the vast majority of these policies are false."

"But based on what? Did he tell you?"

"Signor Aliyan is very well versed in statistics, and it appears there is something highly improbable about the way Signor Bonci's clientele is distributed. There are, for example, the exact same number of people born in January, February, March and so on. Each month has the same number of births. There are twenty-year-olds, forty-year-olds and sixty-year-olds in equal measure. According to Aliyan, that's impossible, or almost. It's as if these policies were deliberately fabricated."

The inspector continued to nod pensively.

It was the same thing that Aliyan had told him. And it made sense. Reality is not a sticker album. There are always fluctuations and deviations.

Where do two lines meet? In a point, Saverio. And that point was the position of Signor Giuseppe Bonci.

Who on Saturday evening had been sitting next to Signor D'Ancona.

"Who poured the wine and the water, do you remember? Was it the waiters, or did the butler deal with it?"

"At the beginning of dinner, it was Bartolomeo personally who filled the glasses. After that, people generally served each other. In fact, now that you've raised the subject, and seeing that it's getting colder, with your permission, what would you say to a nice glass of brandy?"

"Go ahead, Signor Artusi. I'm on duty. Shall I send for Bartolomeo?"

"Please, I'm still able to serve myself. And besides, after what we've just been talking about, forgive me, but I'd rather nobody came anywhere near my glass."

The inspector looked at Artusi with a half-smile. "It seems to me, my dear Signor Pellegrino Artusi, that your brain is still functioning very well."

"That it is," Artusi said, walking over to the drinks cabinet. "That it is, thank God. It's other parts of the body that no longer function quite so well. I'm from Emilia-Romagna, as you know, and for us there are two important things in life." Artusi opened the cabinet and took out a glass bottle full of amber-coloured liquid and a glass. "Fortunately, the stomach still functions, and that's good."

"Don't tell me you no longer enjoy life, Signor Pellegrino."

"On the contrary. I enjoy it more than ever, I can assure you."

"You see? You, Signor Artusi, are one of those for whom the glass is always half full."

"Do you think so?" Pellegrino Artusi slowly turned the glass, watching the amber-coloured liquid descend in gentle arcs.

He had had many things from life. Money, good books, food. Other things he had never had: the peace of a family. He had had a father, a mother, seven sisters. No wife and no children, at least as far as he knew. Not that he could be entirely sure.

There was a girl who had been in the service of his parents, and whom he would visit at night. Then he had left on business, and when he had returned, three months later, the girl was no longer there. Dismissed. She was a shameless hussy, his mother had said. And then she had said something that he had never forgotten.

Anyway, it's better this way. If you'd seen how big she'd got . . .

Pellegrino Artusi held the glass up to the light coming from the window. "Sometimes it's half empty, Ispettore, and sometimes it's half full. It all depends on what's in it."

6

List of facts so far ascertained

Ispettore Artistico took a deep breath, stood up from the chair, put down the sheet of paper and started to walk around the table. Then he sat down again.

The list might turn out to be quite long, but it had to be done. It was impossible to understand a thing otherwise.

1) Everardo D'Ancona died in a room on the second floor with the door locked from the inside.

2) Mantegazza maintains that said door was not opened during the night, as evidenced by the draught excluder that was behind the door (confirmed by Gazzolo and the butler Bartolomeo).

3) It is not possible to gain access to the room any other way.

4) No letter was sent by Signor D'Ancona to the offices in Milan and Rome (not even by ordinary mail, as confirmed by telegram from said offices).

5) The trading licence intended for Giuseppe Bonci was removed surreptitiously from Signor D'Ancona's room.

The inspector looked at point number 5 and nodded gravely. Not mislaid but removed. That letter had been there when Signor D'Ancona had arrived at the castle of Campoventoso, he was now certain of it.

He had found it himself a few hours earlier.

"Ladies and gentlemen, before anything else I want to extend my apologies for having detained you here in the castle well beyond the time you had planned."

Ispettore Artistico, standing with his feet on the floor and his buttocks comfortably propped on the edge of the desk, turned his gaze to those present. As he did so, he pocketed the list of ascertained facts which he had finished a little while earlier. He knew it by heart anyway.

Nobody made any move to protest, even though each one was probably seething inside.

"As you can imagine, the circumstances have required it. That is, they have required me to question all of you one by one, and separately. Having concluded my investigations here, and having acquired all the necessary documentary evidence, I am therefore happy to tell you that as of now you are free to go."

Those present looked at each other, in couples. Only Bonci, instead of looking around, kept his eyes fixed on the inspector.

"Ispettore, if you'll allow me . . ."

"Go ahead, Signor Bonci."

"You say you've acquired all the evidence. Am I to deduce from this that you may possibly have found—"

"The document that interests you, yes. The licence that authorises trade between your insurance company and the Ottoman Empire."

Bonci smiled, the smile of a child who is bought another ice cream after he dropped the first one. "Then tell me, when can I have it back?"

"Aren't you curious to know where it was found?"

Bonci continued to smile. "Shall I tell you the truth? No. That

147

document is of vital importance to me. Even if you'd found it in the pigsty, what matters is that you found it."

"I didn't find it in the pigsty, Signor Bonci, I can assure you of that. I found it in the mail bag." Ispettore Artistico took a large envelope from the desk and held it up in his right hand. "Yesterday, after arriving, I had the good luck to intercept the postman and I asked him to hand over to me all the outstanding correspondence that had been sent from the castle during Sunday. The licence was in this envelope addressed to your house."

"I don't understand, Ispettore. There was no reason for Signor D'Ancona to send me the licence."

Artistico turned the envelope so that the back of it faced outwards and slowly shook his head. "Actually, he didn't send it to you. I said that the letter was addressed to your house, not that it was addressed to you. The letter was addressed to your daughter Delia."

"I . . . Aliyan, do you understand any of this? Why did Signor D'Ancona send that document to my daughter?"

The Turk, both his hands in his pockets, shook his head vigorously in denial. "You must be joking. Signor D'Ancona would never have sent such an important document by post, Bonci *effendi*."

"I'm not joking about this thing, Aliyan. If it wasn't Signor D'Ancona, it must have been someone who had access to his documents." Bonci continued looking at the inspector as he spoke. "Someone who entered his room, for example, perhaps when he was already dead."

"Ispettore, this is slander! I demand that you—"

"Calm down, Signor Aliyan," said Artistico in an icy voice. "You cannot demand anything of me. And you calm down, too, Signor Bonci. It can't have been Signor Aliyan who sent that letter. If you want to take a closer look at the envelope, you will immediately see that the hand that wrote the address is that of a woman."

Bonci was no longer smiling as he took the envelope gingerly in his hand. But his face grew even worse once he had examined the address. He looked as if he were experiencing an attack of congestion.

Perhaps because of the ice cream we spoke of earlier.

"But . . . Delia, this . . ."

Or perhaps because he had recognised the handwriting.

᷍᷍

"Delia! But how . . . but what . . ."

Ispettore Artistico cleared his throat. "You were right, Signor Bonci. The licence was purloined by someone who got into Signor D'Ancona's room. But it wasn't Aliyan who took it, it was your daughter."

"Delia?" said Viterbo. "Excuse me, Ispettore, but when exactly would young Delia have entered Signor D'Ancona's room?"

"When exactly, I don't know. She ought to be able to tell us that, don't you think, signorina?"

Delia Bonci took her eyes – eyes full of tears – away from the tips of her shoes and fixed them on the inspector's eyebrows. Tight-lipped, she shook her head.

"Delia, my dear, don't be afraid. The inspector only wants—"

"And don't call me my dear, you fat, ugly, disgusting man!"

"But . . . Delia . . ."

"Delia, Delia . . . Delia my foot! All you're good for is saying Delia here, Delia there, Delia do this and Delia do that. I hate you, don't you understand? I hate you!"

"But, Delia, I thought—"

"What did you think? That I was dying to get married? To leave home, where my father bosses me about, so that I could be bossed about by a stranger? To then be shown off like a flower in a centrepiece when we go out to dinner? My Delia do this, my Delia do this other thing?" Delia turned to look at her father, pale-faced, her red eyes devastated by tears and mascara. She looked less like a devoted daughter than the bass player of Kiss. "Yes, Papa, I went into Signor D'Ancona's room to get the licence, after I heard about what had happened."

"And how did you do that, signorina?" The inspector's voice was calm.

Hearing that voice, even Delia tried to control herself. Her hands clutched at her dress, crumpling it, but her voice when she spoke was firm. "I heard voices from my room. They were talking about Signor D'Ancona, about how they would have to move the body. That was when I realised that Signor D'Ancona was dead. So I opened the door quietly, just so that I could look in."

She pointed at Bartolomeo with her little finger, palm facing upwards, and then turned her wrist in the gesture of locking a door.

"I saw the butler lock the door, and then I saw him put the key in the cabinet next to the door."

Delia stopped and looked at the inspector, as if waiting for a prompt. Gradually her hands had slowed down.

"Please go on, signorina."

Delia nodded and continued. "So I waited for him to go, I opened the door, I searched and I found the key. Then I went in. I knew where Signor D'Ancona kept the licence. I took it. But while I was there . . ."

"While you were there, someone else came in, didn't they?" This was Gazzolo's voice.

"I heard someone knocking and calling Signor D'Ancona. I took fright and hid under the bed. My heart was in my mouth. I was so scared, I passed out."

"You mean you fainted?" This was Mantegazza's voice.

She nodded and took a deep breath. "Then I heard the door slam and came to. I was about to leave but I heard footsteps from outside, and a woman's voice complaining. I waited a little while longer until the voice disappeared in the distance. Then I left."

"But why did you do it?"

This was the question that Delia had been dreading the most. "I heard that Signor D'Ancona had died, as I told you. And I knew there would be complications. With Signor D'Ancona gone, his colleague Signor Aliyan would never have issued that licence."

"It seems to me you know a lot of things, Signorina Delia."

"My father had told me that Signor Aliyan was against the agreement. If it had been up to him, he would never have released such a document."

"And did your father also know where Signor D'Ancona kept this licence?"

Bonci turned red, which made him look even more like a watermelon. "Ispettore, you're not insinuating that I instructed my daughter to steal—"

"No, Signor Bonci. You didn't know where the licence was, that's obvious. It must have been someone else, don't you think? Someone very, very close to Signor D'Ancona. And close also to you, Signorina Delia."

Bonci's face turned even riper. Now the inspector was insinuating something truly shameful.

"Did you, Signor Aliyan, ever talk privately about this matter with Signorina Delia?"

Before the watermelon could rot, Bonci puffed air into his cheeks. "Ispettore, careful what you say. My daughter does not converse in private with just anyone."

"I understand your reaction, Signor Bonci, but we are talking about serious offences, and there are some people here who haven't told me everything. For example, Signor Aliyan didn't tell me that he specifically asked for a room different from the one that had been assigned to him."

"It didn't strike me as important," said Aliyan. "But yes, I did ask for my room to be assigned to Signor D'Ancona. It was too warm for me."

"And you immediately accepted the first room you were offered?"

"Frankly, I don't remember. But I remember asking for an east-facing room. Because of the light."

"Because of the light. I see. Not because the room was next to that of Signorina Delia?"

Aliyan shrugged. "I don't even know where the signorina's room is."

"Strange, because you spent Saturday night in that room."

Frankly, it would take quite other literary skills to adequately describe the atmosphere in the room following the inspector's words, so we shan't even try.

The only thing we can say is that, while Bonci turned pale, beside him Viterbo suddenly went red in the face. It was as if the blood had moved from one to the other through a pump under the floor.

Then Bonci, almost without moving a muscle of his face, moved his voice. "No-no-no-no. Repeat that, if you're brave enough."

"You heard perfectly well what I said. Signor Aliyan, do you have anything to add?"

"Of course! It's false, absolutely absurd!"

"Signor Bonci, I think Signor Aliyan is able to speak for himself."

"Who told you?"

Aliyan said these words in a calm, almost curious tone. After saying them, he went to Delia and put his arms around her. She responded by clinging to him as if fearing that someone might pull her away.

"A chambermaid discovered you. She smelled your perfume on the sheets, Signor Aliyan, when she was doing the room."

"Yes. It's true, Signor Bonci, and all of you. Delia and I love each other."

Delia confirmed this by nodding vigorously, although she continued to look down.

"We have loved each other for some time, but last night was the first time we'd been together. I think this folly of ours was the reason for Delia's ill-considered and very courageous action. Delia knew that I disapproved of the agreement being ratified, and that I would never have issued the licence. But she also knew where the licence was. That was careless on my part."

Aliyan looked at Delia, who returned the diplomat's hope-green gaze. Then he nodded imperceptibly.

"Yesterday, she briefly confessed to me that she had removed the document and put it in a safe place. She intended to give it back only when he had consented to our marriage."

"Marriage? You can forget about that. Signorina Delia Bonci, who happens to be my daughter, is engaged to Signor Corrado Viterbo. We concluded the agreement last night."

"One moment, one moment, Signor Bonci," Signor Viterbo said, his colour having in the meantime become almost normal again, although his voice still trembled. "I hope you don't think our agreement is still valid."

"But my dear Signor Viterbo, of course it's valid. Surely you're not going to believe a maiden's foolish, sentimental—"

"No longer such a maiden, if I am to believe my ears," Viterbo said, trying to contain himself.

"You can dismiss that, Signor Viterbo. What do you think happened? They will have confided in one another, that's only natural, they're young. But if you want my opinion, I know my daughter, and I know you, if you'll just listen to me . . ."

Signor Viterbo exploded.

Not physically – no, that would have taken weeks to clean up and Crocetta would have had plenty to complain about. But the noise was comparable.

"Listen to you? Listen to you?" Viterbo began screaming. "I've listened to you far too long! What is all this business about the licence? Does a foppish Turk have to tell me that they wanted to deny you a trading licence? I'm going back to Florence now, and I'll check through your papers again, one by one. I should have done it a lot earlier, I should have, but I was blinded by other things! And what will I find in those papers, eh, Signor Bonci?"

"Nothing untoward, Signor Viterbo, trust me. There won't be any problems. Don't listen to these people, I know the situation."

"He knows the situation. Do me a favour! The Turks arrive, they roger your daughter every which way right under your very nose and you claim you're in control of the situation. You're not even in control of your own front door . . ."

And it was at the front door that Viterbo broke off. Not so much out of politeness, to clean his feet before entering someone else's house, as much as because Signor Reza Kemal Aliyan had come right up to him and with an angry but biomechanically efficient gesture had landed him a slap with the back of his hand.

Signor Viterbo was stunned for a moment; then, having taken the Turk by the shoulders with both hands, he headbutted him.

A fight ensued: a fight devoid of style, a mixture of the diplomat's karate and the banker's sumo, while the onlookers, amid a lot of screaming and shoving, tried to separate the adversaries.

In the confused, strident overlapping of voices in the middle of the room, even a poor journalist would have found it quite difficult to get his head around it. The best we can do, therefore, is to propose to the reader a little parlour game. Below is a significant sample of the sentences and interjections heard with greatest clarity and discrimination, and it will be left to the reader to assign an owner to each voice.

The sentences, in chronological order, were:

1) Oh, look, here comes the Sultan. I curse the day I got mixed up with the Turks.

2) I'm not the Turks (incomprehensible phrase). I have a name. You always think like this, you bloody colonialists! You want our money, but not us.

3) What money? You're on your uppers, and if we didn't lend you money . . .

4) Oh, yes, you lend them money! (female sob) They take your money at five per cent, and lend it at twenty.

5) It's the same old story. The people in the bank do all right, the people outside kick the bucket.

6) You should trust us, don't fleece people who work!

7) And you should give back the money you've borrowed from them. Borrowed. That means I give it to you and then you give it back, have you got that or should I say it in Turkish?

8) Calm down, Signor Viterbo, calm down. You see what happens when you trust people who aren't like us?

9) Trust? Trust? You can go to hell, you and your trust! And don't try to butter me up. You've already conned me once, you're not going to tell me now that you're pregnant, are you?

In the commotion, or rather in the general chaos, only a few people managed to stay calm: Bartolomeo, thanks to his long experience; Artusi, insofar as he basically had no stake in the matter; and Ispettore Artistico, who was not so much calm as thoughtful.

What the inspector was thinking about was the sixth fact ascertained on his list, the one that made all this bedlam pointless and put everything that had happened in the past few days into perspective.

6) *The expert chemist Professore Schiff has ruled out the presence of curare, alkaloids or other toxic substances in the victim's stomach and blood.*

In other words, no poison.

Aggravated theft, attempted fraud, exploiting the vulnerable, offences to modesty and common sense, and, in the last quarter of an hour, also a certain number of acts of calumny, slander and blasphemy.

But no murder.

At least not by poisoning.

***

Ispettore Artistico looked again at his list.

3) *It is not possible to gain access to the room in any other way.*

The inspector let his gaze wander around the room, which at that moment looked more like Asterix's village than the castle of

Campoventoso, and thought again about what Delia Bonci had said when he had questioned her. There is a secret passage, with God knows what inside it, though it must be something dangerous, which leads God knows where.

It is not possible to gain access to the room in any other way.

Are we quite sure?

Twice pi

"Good evening, Signor Gazzolo. Before anything else, I hope you are well."

"I'll be better when this whole business is over," Gazzolo replied laconically, touching the large purple bruise on his forehead, the result of an involuntary thrust of an elbow, perhaps from the Turk, perhaps from someone else, while he had been trying to separate the adversaries.

"Yes, I understand you. Though I should point out that some people came out of it worse than others."

"Certainly," Gazzolo said with a little smile, thinking of Bonci. The master of the house, reacting instinctively, had in fact landed a family-size punch on the person closest to him at that moment, in other words, the poor accountant, who had ended up down on the carpet. "I'm sorry. What do you have to ask me that's so important?"

"Some new things have emerged about the death of D'Ancona. I've had a communication from the laboratory of chemical analysis in Florence, which has not discovered any poison in Signor D'Ancona's body."

"You suspected that Signor D'Ancona had been poisoned?"

"It was the only hypothesis I had. You see, Signor Gazzolo, I was starting from the supposition that nobody could have entered his room during the night. I'd assumed this because the door was locked from the inside and there was a draught excluder pushed right up against it. But there are two possible ways in which someone could have got in."

"Yes, I'd thought of that, too," replied Gazzolo, with a slight grimace. "It's possible that someone got in, did what he wanted to do and then went out and pulled the draught excluder with a thread that was inside it until it was right up against the door."

"That's the first way. But there's a second possible way. I ask you because you're the master of the house, Signor Gazzolo: is there a hidden way of gaining access to the room?"

Secondo Gazzolo raised his eyebrows. "Are you asking me if there's a secret passage inside the castle leading to that room?"

"Precisely."

"Absolutely not. There's no secret passage inside the castle."

"What about the door in the wall on the east side? Where does that lead?"

"What door on the east side?"

"The one you frequently use wearing a fencing mask."

Secondo Gazzolo looked at the inspector for a moment, with a bewildered air.

Then he burst out laughing. A real belly laugh, complete with tears in the eyes, the kind that overcomes you and relieves the tensions of the day.

This is no laughing matter, Ispettore Artistico would have liked to say, but it was obvious that it was a laughing matter as far as the master of the house was concerned.

"Excuse me," Gazzolo said, wiping away a tear. "Who told you about the cellar?"

~ast~

At that very moment, while the inspector and the master of the house were merely talking about it, Signor Bonci was acting on it. He had found the door easily: on the wall facing east, as Delia had said, a few metres below the window of her room. That room where . . . No, let's not think about that. Right now, you have to think about yourself, Giuseppe.

Signor Bonci massaged his jaw, where he had been punched a few hours earlier, during all that chaos. You see what happens when you try to keep the peace, Giuseppe? From now on, let's mind our own business and forget about the others. Apart from anything else, we're in a tricky situation. The inspector suspects us. That much is obvious from the questions he asked. The insurance thing we can deal with. He doesn't have anything, only suspicions. But we didn't kill anyone, did we, Giuseppe? There's only one way to get out of this.

Find the secret passage. The tunnel that had been used to surreptitiously enter D'Ancona's room, may he rest in peace, and take his life. That way, he would be able to go to the inspector and put all his cards on the table. And now what shall we do, Ispettore? Seeing that nobody poisoned D'Ancona, Ispettore? What do we do now, Ispettore?

Giuseppe Bonci felt behind the hedge with his hand and immediately hit on the object he was looking for. Slowly, his arm came out into the open, his hand tight around a wooden peg.

Good. Now where?

There was a hole in the wall, square in shape. Exactly the same shape as the peg. Cautiously, his heart pounding, Giuseppe Bonci inserted the peg in the opening.

The door snapped open.

Giuseppe Bonci took a deep breath. As if he had found the *finis Africae*.

Then he placed his hand on the door and went in.

"Conte Pepoli was particularly proud of the cellar, and he was right. It may originally have been a tunnel allowing the count's ancestors to escape, but I don't think it had been used in that way for centuries. Already in the count's day it was being used to store wine, and it is ideal for that purpose. It's spacious, carved out of the rock, has a constant temperature and perfect humidity. That's why the produce from my vineyard is kept there. But believe me, it doesn't lead anywhere."

"Why on earth do you wear a fencing mask when you go in there?"

"It's a simple precaution. You see, I'm a great lover of champagne, and some years ago I started to produce sparkling wine. Unfortunately, one of my workers didn't fully remove the yeast from the bottles of a batch. Do you know what that means?"

Artistico had grown up in a bakery and knew very well what yeast does. It ferments. That is, it transforms complex sugars into simple sugars, and these simple sugars into alcohol and gas. Lots and lots of gas. In bread and cheese, this gas makes holes, in bottles it's there as pressure.

"I see. There must be an enormous amount of pressure inside these bottles."

"Precisely. But we don't know in which ones. Sometimes the cork pops out of one of them. A couple of times it's happened at night, but it usually happens by day, when there's someone there. My estate manager once got hit by a cork just below the ridge of his brow and almost lost an eye. That was very nearly the most serious accident that's occurred since I've been here."

"Because of the cork from a bottle of sparkling wine?"

"A cork like that shoots out at the speed of a rifle bullet. I assure you that wherever it hits you it hurts terribly, but if you get it in the eye, it may cause irreparable damage. That's why anyone entering the cellar must wear a fencing mask. It's a safety procedure I myself introduced."

"And is there no way of distinguishing the faulty bottles from the safe ones?"

"Alas, you'd have to see if the yeast is still there. The only way to see it would be to shake the bottle, but I can assure you that wouldn't be a sensible move. These bottles react to the slightest vibration. I think that's why the corks pop out more often when there's someone in the room."

By now, Signor Bonci had made his way into the cellar inch by inch. Because that's what this damned room was. A cellar, damp and above all dark. You couldn't see a damned thing. Why hadn't he brought a lamp with him? On top of that, it appeared to be an enclosed space. Perhaps there was some other way in or out, but it was impossible to find it in the dark. Or perhaps it was only a cellar.

Signor Bonci looked at the wall in front of him. A blank wall of bottles, placed carefully in their pigeonholes, looked stolidly back at him.

There's nothing here, Giuseppe. Nothing.

Disappointed and annoyed – in fact, downright angry – Signor Bonci struck the wall with his hand.

"By the way, you haven't yet told me who told you about the cellar."

"It was Signor Bonci. His daughter saw you go in there on Saturday afternoon."

"Yes, you're right. And please forgive me, Ispettore, I'm not trying to teach you your job, but isn't it imprudent of you to let someone in on the state of your investigation?"

"You're the master of the house, Signor Gazzolo. I don't see who else I could ask."

"My butler, for example."

"Of course, you're right. But your butler doesn't have an alibi confirmed by two people, one of whom I trust blindly, which places him a long way from Signor D'Ancona's room for the whole of the time the murder would have taken."

Signor Gazzolo nodded and took a large cigar from his breast pocket. Slowly he stood up and walked over to the fireplace. "My butler does have an alibi, you know."

"I don't think I'm jeopardising my investigation too much, Signor Gazzolo, if I tell you that it's certainly not your butler I suspect."

Secondo Gazzolo bit off the tip of the cigar and spat it into his palm. Then he lit the cigar, taking an ember from the fire with the tongs. "And I shan't be so tactless as to ask you who is the person at the centre of your thoughts."

Partly because we both know it's Signor Bonci.

~☆~

"Signorina, I need to have a few words with your father. Do you know where I could find him?"

"I think he's in his room."

"I just tried knocking and there was no answer."

"Oh."

"Do you have any idea where he might have gone?"

"No, I really don't. Are you sure he's not in his room?"

"Nobody opened the door."

"That's strange."

It's more than strange, it's suspicious.

⤸⤷

"Bartolomeo . . ."

"Yes, Ispettore?"

"Have you seen Signor Bonci about?"

"The last time was a few hours ago, Ispettore. In the drawing room. You were there, too."

"And you haven't seen him since then?"

"No, Ispettore. Have you tried his room?"

"Yes, a few minutes ago."

"Would you like me to ask the servants to look for him, sir?"

"Yes, thank you, Bartolomeo."

"Don't mention it, sir."

Even though I think it's a bit late now.

"What was that, sir?"

"Look for him, Bartolomeo, and get the others to look for him. Not only in the castle, everywhere. On the estate and in the fields."

"Do you fear that . . .?"

"Yes, Bartolomeo. I fear that our dear Signor Giuseppe Bonci has run away."

⤸⤷

In reality, Signor Bonci was neither inside the castle nor outside, but under it: in the cellar, motionless.

The blow that Bonci had given the wall with his hand had, in fact, triggered the 140 bottles of sparkling wine he had in front of him, and immediately, nature, in the form of pressure, had given the firing squad the order to shoot.

The cork from a bottle of sparkling wine can reach 90 kilometres an hour: not quite as fast as a bullet, which travels ten times faster, but all the same. An object weighing ten grams that hits you at 900 kilometres an hour will kill you; an object weighing ten grams that hits you at 90 kilometres an hour won't necessarily kill you, but it certainly won't improve your well-being.

The first cork had hit Giuseppe Bonci on the neck; the second, straight in one eye. The third got him right in the balls, a word which, even though it may seem strange to some, already existed at the beginning of the last century, and even then, if you were hit in them, it hurt quite a lot.

Then the poor man had lost count, mercilessly targeted by that improvised submachine gun of compressed air, until a particularly charitable cork had hit him slap bang in the right temple, and at that point he lost consciousness, ending up on the floor amid the corks, while all around him the open bottles merrily sprayed the confined space and everything that was inside. Including Signor Giuseppe Bonci, who was not found until two hours later, unconscious and soaked in sparkling wine.

7, I think

"How are you, Signor Bonci?"

"Bad, by God, bad."

Anyone who was a real bastard would have pointed out to Signor Bonci that this was a violation of the second commandment, but at that moment Ispettore Artistico was not driven by feelings of revenge.

"I'm aching all over, Ispettore. And I only did it to help you, do you know that?"

"I know, Signor Bonci. You were inspecting the cellar to see if you could get into one of the rooms of the castle."

"That's right, Ispettore." Bonci nodded gravely, looking at the inspector with a wild eye. Best to say "eye", in the singular, not out of a liking for synecdoche – although this would be perfectly fine in a novel from the beginning of the last century – but for love of the truth: Bonci's left-hand visual organ was closed beneath a swollen and purple eyelid, and the man had only his right eye with which to look out at the world.

"You took quite a big risk, Signor Bonci. And you gave us quite a big fright."

"Then imagine how frightened I was. Was it you who found me?"

"Bartolomeo and I together."

"And you went right inside the cellar? I didn't get anywhere, but I was in the dark. Maybe with a light . . ."

"I inspected the place inch by inch, even though Signor Gazzolo had already gone before me. That passage used to lead to the drawing room, it was an escape route in mediaeval times, but it's been closed up for centuries. It doesn't lead anywhere."

"Ispettore . . ."

"I'm here, Signor Bonci."

"Keep looking for that damned secret passage, Ispettore. You have to find it. It all revolves around that, mark my words."

Ispettore Artistico looked straight into Bonci's remaining good eye. It was wild, watery and feverish. The man wasn't well.

"Let me deal with it. For now, you have to rest. I'll send Dottore Mantegazza to you right away."

～ン～

"Well, Professore?" asked Crocetta. "How is Signor Bonci?"

"How is Signor Bonci?" Mantegazza asked himself, shaking his head. "He had an unpleasant misadventure. Palpebral and periorbital oedema in the left eye and bruises all over his body."

"He also took quite a blow in the temple, I saw," said Crocetta, continuing to walk beside Mantegazza, holding his doctor's bag.

"Yes, but that's not what worries me," Mantegazza replied assertively. "There are no signs of concussion."

"Maybe. To me it sounded like he was rambling. He kept talking about secret passages. It must be the fever."

"His temperature's normal. He doesn't have a fever."

"Then why's he raving?"

"Oh, that's the most interesting thing. He's blind drunk."

"Drunk? But why? Did he drink while he was in—"

"No, not at all. But he was immersed in alcoholic liquid for a couple of hours. Ethyl alcohol is easily able to penetrate the skin. In this way it soon enters the bloodstream and the altered state that ensues lasts much longer."

"Oh, my. I didn't know that."

You see how many things you learn when you're with people who really know their stuff. And she had been quite pleased to assist Mantegazza while he examined the sick man. Now, though . . .

"Now, Professore, if you don't mind, I have to get back to work."

"We've finished, Crocetta, thank you. Do you have a lot to do?"

She took a deep breath. "Well, I'm not idle."

In fact, having finished playing nurse, Crocetta was now expected to join Bartolomeo and the rest of the staff in mopping up after the disaster in the cellar. Then at last she would be able to do her work: that is, wash the towels stained with pomegranate juice, which doesn't go away even when you pray to the Virgin or curse all the Saints one after the other. The only way was to make a little soap, the common or garden kind, with lard and caustic soda: that was why she had gone to the cellar in the first place, to get the good lard, which was almost odourless. And then she would have to make it outside, in the cold: if Gazzolo caught her using caustic soda in the house, at the very least he would dismiss her. About such things, the master was uncompromising. Like wearing a mask when you went to the cellar.

"How many hours a day do you work, Crocetta?"

"That's an easy sum to do, Professore. The hours I don't sleep. And lately I haven't been getting much sleep anyway."

"That's an injustice, don't you think? People forced to work like that for so many hours, beyond the limits of their physical capacities. It's inhuman."

Mantegazza shook his head as he opened the door to his own room.

"It's something I've been saying for a long time now in my books, but it's not enough to stir people's consciences. I think it's time I did something in parliament. Where civility cannot reach, the law must step in. Thank you."

Mantegazza took his bag from the maid's hands and placed it on the bed.

"But it isn't easy, you know. It isn't easy. The wheels of parliament grind exceedingly slowly, and in the end all the energy is expended on pointless friction between the parts of the mechanism instead of getting the mechanism to work."

Is that so? Interesting.

"And what would be in this law of yours?"

Obligatory limits to the hours of work? Less inhuman conditions?

"The chief proposal would be to distribute free to workers of the lower classes an appropriate daily dose of coca leaves, which they could chew regularly, so that they could attend to their duties with greater vigour."

And there was I, imagining I wouldn't have to work so hard. What a fool I was.

※

"Here I am, Bartolomeo. Sorry I'm late, but I had to assist Professore Mantegazza in examining Bonci."

Holy Mother of God, what a mess! The cellar was a tangle of bottles, some full, some empty, some intact, some in pieces, and the air was saturated with a smell that went to your head. Bartolomeo, who was sweeping enough shards of glass to fill a barrow, nodded without raising his head.

"Anyway, our problems are over, Bartolomeo. The professor says he's bringing in a law to drug us all like turkeys, so that we can work twenty-four hours a day. But given that the law hasn't been introduced yet, we have to do what we can with the strength we've got. Where should I start?"

"We can manage here, Crocetta, thank you," Bartolomeo

replied, his head still bent over the shards. "Go to see Signora Clara, she's expressly asked for you."

"Oh. Alright. If you're sure that—"

"I think it's more urgent that you go to the signora, Crocetta."

Why wouldn't Bartolomeo look her in the eye?

~☙~

"Yes, who is it?"

"It's the chambermaid, Signor Viterbo."

"Ah. Just a minute."

Corrado Viterbo took his jacket from the back of the chair and his trousers from the bed. His dignity might have gone down the pan before now, but being seen by the chambermaid in his underwear was a step too far.

"You can come in now."

Crocetta opened the door and came in, sniffling. "Excuse me, Signor Viterbo. The signora has sent me to ask if you need anything."

Viterbo, standing by the mirror, looked at her.

Do I need anything? Of course I do. But I don't know what. I'm well off, in fact I'm decidedly rich. I have a fine house and a good job. I have everything, but something is missing. Someone is missing. Someone to leave all this to. And someone to talk to about it. I deluded myself, deluded myself that I'd found that someone. But I think I realised that she wasn't actually what I was looking for.

What Corrado Viterbo was suffering from the most, he now realised, wasn't that he had lost Delia. It was the prospect of being alone again. Alone and without any reason to get up in the morning. Which took a great deal of effort even when he was in an excellent mood, so just imagine what it was like when everything seemed black, like now.

"What was that, sir?"

It was only now that Viterbo realised he had been thinking aloud.

"Nothing, nothing. I was simply reflecting on the fact that I have nothing to look forward to."

"If you'd like to swap, sir . . ."

"What do you mean?"

"Nothing, sir. Don't take any notice of me. I talk too much. That's why it happened, you know. I talk too much."

Viterbo looked straight at Crocetta, without the mirror as intermediary. Her eyes were red from crying. "What happened?"

"I've been dismissed, sir. I have to be out of here in a week."

"For what reason?"

"You should know, sir."

"I?"

"For saying that last night the Turkish gentleman . . . you know, sir."

Corrado Viterbo rolled his eyes. "What did you do?"

"I was the one who told the inspector what had happened. I didn't think I could keep it quiet, sir. I knew the signora would disapprove, but it was a question of justice, I couldn't hide what I knew. I beg your pardon, sir."

Viterbo looked at the girl for a couple of seconds, stunned. Then he shook his head slowly, almost smiling. "And why do you need to ask my pardon, pray? You did your duty, that's all."

Crocetta nodded, sniffing. "It'd be nice if everyone thought like you, sir. If you need anything . . ."

"I need to speak with your mistress to tell her what I think of you, my dear Crocetta."

"I don't have a master or a mistress, sir. I've never had any."

From the diary of Pellegrino Artusi

Campoventoso, October 23, 1900

For two or three nights now, I have been sleeping badly, either too much or too little, and at the moment I am not drowsy at all. I just now took my leave of Mantegazza, who struck me as extremely anxious.

Apparently, results have arrived from the civic laboratory, concerning the death of poor Signor D'Ancona, which are quite conclusive. It appears that no trace of poison has been found in the victim's stomach or blood. Which means that Signor D'Ancona was not murdered. Mantegazza, however, seems unable to resign himself, and I genuinely find that hard to understand. That someone should die is quite sad; but if he had been bumped off, that would have been worse. I have the impression that my good friend Mantegazza is more displeased at having seen his own theory confounded than about the misfortune in itself.

But perhaps I am being too harsh on my colleague. I, too, I have to admit, have continued for hours to be troubled by an obsession.

All day my thoughts have kept returning to the dish that Aliyan and I did not have time to prepare, and whose missing recipe torments me. I keep racking my brains to understand how I could combine those elements but am unable to work it out.

I should perhaps feel guilty, I sometimes think. I cannot deny that it was a relief to know that poor Signor D'Ancona passed over to a better life of his own accord, without anyone giving him a push. But, even when I believed that we were involved with a murder, my brain continued to toy with that devilish recipe.

Well, I find it hard to feel guilty. I feel I did my best, talking with the inspector and telling him the truth about what I know, avoiding speculating on what I do not know to him or to others. If we are prepared in what we speak about, our duty is to do something; in the contrary case, where we know nothing, I think our specific duty is to abstain from doing anything at all, certainly not the kinds of things that are done just so as not to appear indifferent.

This society of ours would work a lot better if everyone made an effort to do what he can to the best of his ability, tried to learn what he cannot do, and remembered, wherever he is, the difference between these two things. As the great Socrates says: "I know only one thing: that I know nothing." It may be only one thing, but it is a great thing. I am not Socrates, and in fact I delude myself that I know a few things. One, above all, I know: I know how to cook and how to eat. That seems quite a small thing, but it is not.

❧

This hypocritical world does not want to accord any importance to eating, but then there are no festivals, civil or religious, where we do not lay the table and try to guzzle as much as we can. Indeed, as we did here, finding it only natural to ratify a trade agreement with the empire of the Turks with a fine spread.

I am convinced that this apparently humble practice can promote mutual respect between nations. Because we all eat, and we can all appreciate and understand each other's cuisine. If you put a Turkish or Chinese person in front of me and they declaim to me the most elevated poetry in their language, well, I would not understand a thing; but if you put in front of me a dish of theirs, whether it be of meat or fish or vegetables, I am *perfectly able to eat it and derive nourishment from it, and perhaps also pleasure. Cookery is a universal language, which needs to be understood only by those who practise it: perhaps only music is its equal. And yet, one can spend days, weeks, whole months without listening to melodies, but try to go a day without eating! We can philosophise as much as we like, but if we all want to be well, it is necessary to start, not from the things that would improve us as long as we could do them, but from those things which we cannot do without. Today we have fuel-driven automobiles, steam trains, carriages with horses, wagons and bicycles; and yet, none of these would exist if we did not have . . . the wheel, some might think. No, I say the hub. The humble pivot that is not seen, and around which the wheel, the undisputed foundation of human inventiveness, turns, transmitting the motion that something else generates. If this element did not exist, or if it were weak, we would not go anywhere.*

If we . . .

Pellegrino Artusi stopped with his pen in mid-air.

Not because he didn't know what to write. But because of the noise.

7 for real

That night, nobody had found it easy to fall asleep.

It wasn't simple; the wind was howling even more loudly than usual and blowing through all the flues of the castle, sounding like a gigantic organ and inspiring in the guests, instead of celestial aspirations, rather more earthly preoccupations. That was why almost nobody was asleep in the castle that night.

～✦～

Signora Clara was awake beside her husband, although he was snoring heartily.

Imagine that. It would take more than a dead man under his roof and fraud on an international scale to deprive Secondo of his sleep. And now that the inspector has told him that nobody helped Signor D'Ancona to die . . . That's what Secondo is like: if something doesn't directly concern him, it might as well not exist. The same with the upkeep of the house. It's a good thing I'm here to take care of it. That little busybody. Oh, but I put you in your place. The usual week, and then you're out of here. Where did she think she was? Servants have always gossiped. But among themselves. Not to the police, oh no. Well, she won't do that again.

～✦～

Crocetta was awake, looking by the light of the candle at her little room on the floor below.

You don't have a bath, you don't have electric light, you don't have a fire. It's terrible. Not that it matters, Crocetta. You have to get out of here anyway. They're sending you away. So what? You're not like Bartolomeo, who has roots. You'll find another place. You'll see, you'll find one. Yes, you'll see. I've never liked it here. So why do I feel like crying?

✻

Bartolomeo was awake. He usually fell asleep thinking of the list of things to do the following day, but not tonight.

Bartolomeo was awake, because although it was no longer a case of murder, something unpleasant had nevertheless happened in that house, on his watch. The police had come.

The police, in his house. It had never happened before. It should never have happened at all. It was as close to dishonour as Bartolomeo could imagine, topped only by the possibility of being dismissed.

Bartolomeo was awake, very much awake.

Only when the inspector had gone would Bartolomeo be able to sleep.

✻

Signor Viterbo was awake. Before going to bed he had looked at himself in the mirror for a long time.

What is it you lack, Corrado? What do you need?

✻

Aliyan was awake, writing a letter to Delia. Which is why it would be inappropriate and even a little impolite to reveal what he was thinking about. In some circumstances, a man has a right to remain alone.

⁓✥⁓

Delia was awake, huddled in her sheets beneath which she had taken refuge to lose herself in the perfume of roses and wild musk, without knowing if she was pleased or desperate, proud or mad.

⁓✥⁓

Ispettore Artistico was awake, watching all his mental constructions melt like snow in the sun. Because what Giuseppe Bonci had done, foolish as it was, had been revelatory. Bonci was really convinced that there was a secret passage in the castle. Meaning?

Meaning he was convinced that someone had used that passage to get to Signor D'Ancona's room. The only possible way in without opening the door.

Because that door had not been opened. After leaving Bonci, Artistico had done a few tests on the draught excluder, trying to pull it taut from the outside with a thread, but the very construction of the door made that impossible: the draught excluder was firmly placed, Mantegazza had said, and with the thread the inspector had managed, with some difficulty, only to prop it against the door.

Ditto for the window: opening it from the outside, in the dark, on a ladder that would have had to be several metres high, was simply madness.

Artistico had also looked inside the fireplace, to check that there weren't any grooves that could have been used for climbing. You could come down the chimney like Father Christmas, perhaps, but to get back up you would have to be Diabolik on a diet. Since both were imaginary characters, and neither of the two were known to Europeans in 1900, the inspector had deduced that it wasn't possible to get in that way either.

There remained only one plausible hypothesis.

Signor Everardo D'Ancona had died a natural death, whatever Mantegazza said.

And this prevented Ispettore Saverio Maria Artistico from sleeping.

⚜

In short, almost nobody was asleep that night.

In particular, Signor Giuseppe Bonci couldn't get to sleep and was walking up and down the drawing room with a candle in his hand. It was 1.30 a.m., and everyone was asleep. Or so he thought.

But not him. No, he couldn't get to sleep. And not because of the pains from the wounds, although he had those, especially in the eye, not to mention his lower regions. No, the anxiety that churned Signor Bonci's entrails and thoughts was all internal and had to do with that secret passage. There had to be one somewhere.

There may be those among my readers who think that this obsession of Bonci's was completely insane, and they would be right: a clear-headed person in full possession of his faculties, after touching with his hand, so to speak, the fallacy of his own hypothesis, would have dismissed it.

But Signor Bonci was not clear-headed. He was, to use a technical term, plastered.

As Mantegazza had predicted, it is easy to get drunk through the skin and extremely difficult to sober up. And, as often happens when we're blind drunk, the obsession with the secret passage wouldn't go away either.

The inspector had said that once upon a time the tunnel had ended up in the drawing room. Good. That meant it might start in the drawing room. You just had to look for a secret mechanism.

The wax from the candle dripped onto Bonci's hand, and he gave a start. Then he began to look around, searching for a place to put it. There was a candle holder on the wall next to the fireplace. Bonci placed the candle in it and took advantage of the light to take a good look at the wall, in search of a crack.

Nothing.

Bonci took the candle and placed it in the twin candle holder on the other side of the fireplace. In putting it there his hand encountered something strange.

This candle holder was different. It was as solid as the other, but seemed to have something artificial about it, as if . . . Bonci looked at the wall, and felt his heart miss a beat.

This candle holder was not fixed to the wall. It had been inserted in a slit, as if . . .

As if it were a device.

With enthusiasm in his heart, Signor Bonci pulled on the candle holder with all his might and felt the device click and set off a mechanism, which began turning fast.

To be precise, this mechanism was there to regulate the movements of a one-ton chandelier.

~<del></del>~

The crash was interpreted by the guests of the castle in different ways.

For Pellegrino Artusi and Paolo Mantegazza, that noise echoing through the castle sounded like the earth's crust shifting.

Clearly it was an earthquake, which is why both men rushed out of their rooms with all the agility they could muster, which wasn't much, but hopefully just enough.

☙❧

For Bartolomeo, it had to have been a flash of lightning that had directly hit the inside of the castle, suddenly, without rain or anything else – well, the seasons were no longer what they once had been – but it certainly came from the drawing room. You will pardon the somewhat incoherent reasoning: the poor butler had only just fallen asleep.

☙❧

For Reza Kemal Aliyan, former lieutenant in the Ottoman army, this was quite clearly the noise of an Austro-Hungarian cannon, which is why his first instinct had been to look for his sabre and organise an attack, before realising that he was in a castle in the Tuscan countryside, where in order to have a war, complete with bombardments, it would be necessary to wait another forty years or so.

☙❧

Other hypotheses worthy of note, in everyone's half-waking state, were: the structural collapse of a load-bearing wall; the derailing of the Siena–Arezzo mail train with the castle in place of the blind track; a simultaneous explosion of all the cows on the farm; Armageddon.

Bonci would probably have endorsed this last interpretation, if he had not been the person responsible for all this racket.

"Ooowww . . ."

The door opened, noisily dragging with it a myriad of crystals and pieces of metal, and Bartolomeo's face appeared. Even in the weak light from the candle, it didn't seem nearly as impassive as usual.

"Ooohhh . . ."

Bartolomeo raised the candlestick, casting a downward light on the true proportions of the disaster.

Because it was a disaster.

"Aaahhh . . ."

Bartolomeo cautiously headed towards the moaning, walking around the remains of the chandelier, which lay shattered in the middle of the room, a gigantic artificial jellyfish that had run aground on an expanse of crockery, books and vases.

"Ooooooh . . ."

Bartolomeo moved forward, stepping over one of the heavy oak bookcases that up until a little while earlier had been standing against the wall and now lay face down on the floor.

The moaning came from nearby. Bartolomeo raised the candlestick higher, noting that only the wall to the east had been badly damaged: the one in front, apart from the shards on the floor, seemed intact.

"Urrrgggh . . ."

The chandelier had not in fact crashed straight to the ground, as would have happened if Bonci had pulled with force on both the arms of the candle holder, that is, on both levers of the mechanism. As it was, only the two chains to the north and west had given way, while those to the south and east had remained fixed. This had turned the chandelier into a pendulum which had swung through the room like a wrecking ball, sweeping up everything it found in its path before smashing into the wall, at which point the other two chains had yielded and the monster had finally crashed to the ground.

"Jesus, Mary and Joseph . . ."

Bartolomeo moved the candlestick closer to the fireplace. Nothing that had been in the trajectory of the chandelier had remained intact, not even the two bishops who had been on guard beside the fireplace.

The candle threw a pitiless light on the two wooden church-men, heaped one on top of the other as if in an unlikely, polychrome act of sodomy, Saint François de Sales underneath, seeming to lean on his stick in order to free himself from that obscene situation, and Saint Carlo Borromeo on top with his index finger and middle finger raised, as if celebrating the happy outcome of the long, motionless courtship.

Bartolomeo cautiously stepped down from the bookcase, placing a foot on the floor.

"Aaaaayyyyy . . ."

Or rather, not quite on the floor. Actually, on a hand. A hand attached to an arm protruding from the tangle of wooden limbs, and which the butler in the half-light had taken for one of the bishops.

Bartolomeo, after lifting his foot instinctively, put the candle-stick down on the floor.

Stuck, somewhat askew, between the two wooden prelates, was the rest of Signor Giuseppe Bonci.

～❧～

"How firm Signorina Delia was."

Paolo Mantegazza poured himself a finger of brandy from the bottle and put it down on the side table in Pellegrino Artusi's room.

This was where they found themselves after the big bang, after Signor Bonci had been extricated from the ecumenical embrace of the statues, and after Delia Bonci had taken her father gently by the hand and said:

"Come on, Papa. Let's go to bed."

And so Bonci had gone to bed, while Bartolomeo and the others had readied themselves for a second round of removing rubble caused by the accountant. Mantegazza, after administering a sedative to Signora Clara, had also briefly examined Artusi and Artistico, diagnosed a state of shock and commandeered a bottle of Armenian brandy for therapeutic purposes. The three men had then holed up in Artusi's room and now, what with the smoke from the pipes and the fumes of the brandy, their nerves had indeed calmed somewhat.

"I was completely mistaken, you know, about the signorina," the inspector said. "I thought she was a slyboots, instead of which she has demonstrated uncommon courage."

"Most certainly. She has intelligence and composure, she knows what to do at the right time. I must say I was a little surprised the other day when you abandoned her at the climax of her story."

"When was that, Professore?" the inspector asked.

"When she said she fainted under the bed when Aliyan suddenly entered the room. In such situations, our bodies usually give the best of themselves. It's only later, once the danger has passed, that they abandon us. Instead of which, she fainted at the very moment her heart might have been expected to beat the fastest."

Artusi nodded. He had never been a courageous man. He had a clear memory of the years from 1848 onwards, when the wars of independence devastated the country and he had crossed Italy from south to north, though steering well clear of Milan when the Five Days were at their height. A little while earlier, in the winter of '48, he had found himself in a trattoria in Bologna, at the same table as the anarchist Felice Orsini, who was in quest of proselytes for the insurrections; and while Orsini was stirring up the crowd, searching among those present for someone with the same fanatical look in his eyes as himself, Pellegrino Artusi had sat with his head bent over his plate of macaroni, pretending he wasn't even there. He had been given the nickname "macaroni eater", consoling himself as time passed and he reached the age of eighty that not one member of the company that had applauded Orsini had reached half that milestone.

But his father, knowing that his son was a committed Mazzinian, and having become aware of that dinner, had sent him on a nice little journey far from the troubles. Pellegrino had crossed Italy from Naples to Rome, experiencing spas, plates of spaghetti and provocative landladies with distracted husbands; the one physical consequence had been haemorrhoids, which had proliferated in painful clusters like a war wound, although a lot less heroic.

"Of course, the poor girl must have had a great shock – I've had similar things happen to me," replied Artusi, thinking mainly of those times when the aforementioned husbands had returned home unexpectedly.

The three of them lapsed into silence for a moment, the kind of embarrassed silence you get in a lift when you run out of things to say. Then, slapping his thigh, Mantegazza said:

"Well, Ispettore, tomorrow we'll be saying goodbye."

"Yes, indeed. Tomorrow – or rather, today."

"We can't say it's been a boring weekend," Artusi observed, starting to get to his feet with the air of someone who sees that the time has come to say farewell and is preparing to see the guests to the door.

"No, certainly not."

"But if I may ask . . ." said Mantegazza.

"Go ahead, Professore."

"Are you convinced by the outcome of your investigation?"

The inspector waited a moment before answering. Sometimes we are tempted to answer a question that is different from the one we are asked. It was as if Ispettore Artistico had heard the question as "Are you happy with the outcome of your investigation?" No, Saverio Artistico wasn't in the least happy. Artistico liked to find the culprit, liked to participate in the search for evidence that would nail them, liked to make people admit their guilt.

If guilt there was. But if there wasn't any, it was the specific duty of Ispettore Artistico Saverio Maria to put a stop to the vengeful desires of his namesake Saverio Maria Artistico.

"The thing is, Professore, I only have your word for it that a murder was committed. All the remaining evidence points to the contrary. And if I must be honest, I've forced myself to go beyond the bounds of logic and common sense in my attempt to find a way to get into that damned room."

Ispettore Artistico fell silent, thinking again about when he had looked inside the fireplace for a way to climb up it. Then he opened his hands and spread his palms in a gesture of surrender.

"But what I could humanly do, I have done, and now I can't linger any longer. Even if I could, I don't know if I would want to. The atmosphere is growing heavy, for everyone."

"But you're doing your duty. You're investigating a case of murder."

"Up until a few hours ago, yes. But not anymore. As I've told you, there is no poison in Signor D'Ancona. And there's no way of entering his room without leaving traces. Which means . . ."

Pellegrino Artusi raised his head and put a hand on

Mantegazza's forearm. If it had not been for his whiskers, it would have been visible from a distance that he was open-mouthed.

For the last few minutes, ever since Mantegazza had talked about courage, the mind of the elderly merchant had returned to the year of grace 1848. To his journey from Naples to Rome, and everything he had seen.

And, thinking about it again, he had remembered something he had seen not far from Naples.

"Dear Professore, dear Ispettore," Artusi said, "forgive me for interrupting you, but if I were in Professore Mantegazza's shoes, as a doctor and even more as a representative of the Kingdom, I would be inclined to consider it as murder until light had been thrown on the matter."

The inspector felt the muscles of his neck stiffen.

He hadn't left a life in which you become a criminal by exchanging favours with bandits to become an inspector by exchanging favours with senators.

"I am grateful to you, Signor Artusi, but sooner or later the truth would come out. I am not accustomed to—"

"Ispettore, I have no intention of helping you to temporise. I don't know, I really don't know if Signor D'Ancona was suffocated by someone, but I know how it would be possible to do it. And you yourself, just now, supplied me with a further possibility."

"Signor Artusi, please. We're in an old castle, but that doesn't mean there are ghosts."

"Heaven forbid." Artusi raised his hands. "No ghosts, Ispettore. Only reality, solid reality."

"Things we can touch, you mean?"

"Precisely. Things we can touch."

⁓≫≪⁓

"Professore Mantegazza?"

Artusi had been speaking for about ten minutes, calmly, but trying to keep his voice as low as possible. Artistico had remained motionless, listening, his hands joined in front of his face. Then he had turned and asked:

"Could it work, Professore Mantegazza?"

Mantegazza turned his gaze from his friend to the inspector. "It could, certainly. And not only that. It would explain everything."

"Everything?"

"Everything."

Ispettore Artistico got slowly to his feet. His hands were shaking.

No, it wouldn't explain everything. It wouldn't explain *why*.

You don't kill someone without a motive. And if things happened just the way you say, not only have you told me how Everardo D'Ancona was killed, but also who killed him.

The only person who could have done it.

But given his position, the role he occupies, this would seem to be more an act of madness than a reasoned act.

And the person wasn't mad. He didn't seem mad at all.

With circumspect steps, the inspector walked over to the bookcase and looked at the few volumes there. Every now and again, he would take one out, give it a glance and put it back in its place.

"If you're looking for a secret passage, Ispettore, I fear you won't find it there," Artusi said affably.

The inspector shook his head. "No, my dear Pellegrino, I'm looking for something to read. What you told me is enough to keep one from sleeping. And if I wasn't sleepy earlier, I'm certainly not sleepy now. But I do need to sleep, in order to think clearly. So I was looking for a good tome, something that would waft me into the arms of Morpheus."

Artusi continued to smile, his whiskers like a raised curtain. "Oh, if you're looking for a book that will help you to sleep, I have one that's perfect for you."

From 270 to 176

No. 270. Cauliflower in Bechamel sauce.
The inspector turned the page.

As he read, Artistico was getting more and more rattled. He certainly didn't feel like sleeping.

It probably wasn't Artusi's fault. On the contrary, from what little Artistico could grasp, his book was truly enjoyable. "Here," Artusi had said, handing him a copy of his volume. "It's my personal copy, the first copy printed of the first edition. I never travel without it. It's a kind of talisman. If this doesn't send you to sleep, I should point out that I've also written a biography of the poet Ugo Foscolo."

The inspector had gone to bed and started to leaf through the book. It was the first time in his life that he had read a cookery book.

It certainly hadn't induced sleep.

That night, the words flashed before his eyes, without managing to form sentences, let alone concepts, in his brain – he was too busy trying not to worry about the cosmic mess in which he found himself.

The inspector had gone into the drawing room convinced that he was in a mess and had returned to his own room aware that the mess was much greater than a chandelier.

It was as if he couldn't decide what to think about. That was why he had made up his mind to try and sleep, and to approach the matter with a clear head in the morning.

All cabbages, whether they are white, black, yellow or green,
are the children or stepchildren of Aeolus, god of the winds,
and yet those who have problems with wind recall that
for them these plants are true crucifers, so called because
their flowers bear four petals in the shape of crosses.

Artistico smiled. If he had been calm, he would probably even have started to laugh. How can you talk about farting in a cookbook?

He remembered what Artusi had said to him only a couple of hours earlier. And, increasingly, he was convinced that the old man had hit the target.

If it had happened like that, he would have both the method and the murderer. Of course, two trifles were missing. Firstly: the evidence. Secondly, and much more importantly: the motive.

Saverio Artistico was convinced, however, that this last could be found later. First, the evidence. Of course, it is necessary to understand why one person kills another; but first, even before that, it is absolutely obligatory to demonstrate that he has done so. There may be dozens of motives for murder. The victim himself might have his own motive for making all those he knew yearn for his death. Especially if he was very rich, or very important. If you go after the motive, you find only what you want to look for.

The inspector went further back in the book. And as if by magic he came upon a recipe that reminded him of something.

No. 176. Thrushes with olives.

Ah. The famous recipe that Signor D'Ancona had wanted to hear during that last dinner, God knows why.

Thrushes and other small birds in a stew can be cooked like pigeons (no. 172); in fact, that is the way I recommend you to cook them. Olives softened in salt water are usually added, complete with their stones, when the thrushes are halfway ready. It is better, however, to take out the stone: with a pocketknife, make a ribbon of the pulp, wrapping it in a spiral around itself, so that it appears to form a whole olive.

Once, six thrushes were given as a gift to a gentleman who, since his family was away in the country at that time, thought to take them to a trattoria and have them roasted. They were fine specimens, as fresh and fat as Orphean warblers, and yet, fearing they might swap them for other birds, he marked his by cutting off their tongues. The waiters, growing suspicious, started to examine them to see if any mark appeared and, lo and behold, they were clever enough to find it. In order not to be taken in by his trick, or perhaps because that gentleman was not exactly generous in his tips, "We'll trick him," they cried with one voice; and, having cut the tongues off six of the scrawniest thrushes that were in the kitchen, they prepared those for him, saving his for the customers they cared more about.

Having arrived, our friend, eager for his meal, and seeing his birds looking all dry and skinny, opened his eyes wide and, turning them over and over, said, "I am astonished! Are these really my thrushes?" Then, checking that the tongues were missing, he dolefully told himself that the spit and the fire must have caused the transformation.

To the customers who came later, the first thing the waiters said triumphantly was: "How about a beautiful thrush today?" and they sang the praises of their fine product, as was narrated to me by someone who had eaten them.

The inspector read the recipe two or three times, and the sense of incredulity grew in his chest until it became a symphony, a kind of orchestra of blaring trumpets, while a choir of angels sang: "How lucky you are, Ispettore Artistico."

~⁂~

"Yes? Who's there?"

This was said in a slightly more irritable tone than earlier. True, the older one gets, the lighter one sleeps, but all the same.

"It's me. Artistico."

The lock turned, the door opened, and Pellegrino Artusi appeared in his nightshirt, with leather slippers and a cap with a pompom.

"I need you, Signor Artusi."

"At your service. Please come in."

"No, I need you to get dressed and come with me."

Artusi looked at the inspector somewhat dubiously. I get it that you trust me, but couldn't you have chosen somebody else?

"If you'll just give me a moment . . ."

"Of course. In the meantime, while you get ready, I'll go and call Mantegazza."

"Am I not enough for you?"

"The more of us there are, the better. Trust me."

~⁂~

The inspector had been right. The undertaking had been brief but tiresome. Tiresome for the nerves, having to do everything without waking anyone. And tiresome for the body, because apart from anything else it had required them to wait for the night to convince itself to become dawn, then to leave the castle and go where they had to go with just a modicum of light at their disposal before everyone woke up. It had been bitterly cold and even windier than usual, which was why Mantegazza had demanded that the bottle of brandy in his room be opened again. Partly because of the cold, and partly because of the emotion of what they had discovered, the bottle had tried to resist for half an hour, but had eventually raised the white flag and had been inexorably drained by the three of them, who were now sitting in the inspector's room, looking like old conspirators in a tavern who haven't even noticed that the place has shut for the night.

"I don't think Gazzolo will be pleased," said Mantegazza, turning the bottle upside down and watching a single drop fall to the floor.

"Ah, some have suffered more than he," the inspector said, breathing in with his eyes closed. He wasn't used to drinking brandy, and now the whole room was spinning.

"No, that's true. D'Ancona lost his life. And he didn't even have time to enjoy his new glasses." He sobbed. "He had new glasses, did you know that? Eyeglasses. He told me when I examined him."

"That's why." Artusi shook his head, with watery eyes and an inebriated air. "A lot of things are coming back to me now, you know. Even the fact that the wood didn't catch fire easily. It was damp."

"Yes, of course," Artistico said. "In that cold . . . Talking of fiery things, Pellegrino, did you get the one we were talking about? It's the right one, isn't it?"

"Yes, I think so. When I took it, I was sober."

Artusi reached his hand out to his cloak and pulled from the garment a can bearing the words, in attractive lettering:

AWARD-WINNING GAZZOLO COMPANY –
STEWED BEEF IN SPICY SAUCE

8

"At this hour?"

"Yes, at this hour. What can I tell you?"

Bartolomeo turned the can in his fingers. The meat his master produced. Bartolomeo had never tasted it – as far as he was concerned, eating meat out of a can was not much less indecent than going around with your face painted blue.

"Let's see if I've got this right. Signor Artusi wants this thing warmed up in the kitchen for his breakfast?"

"Not him. Apparently, Dottore Mantegazza ordered him to. Apparently, Signor Artusi didn't sleep too well last night" – with her thumb Crocetta mimed someone drinking straight from the bottle.

"Crocetta, please. Stop making those gestures."

"Why? Because they'll dismiss me? You're a bit late there, Bartolomeo."

"Anyway, none of us slept well last night. Not the masters, and not us."

"What are you doing, changing the subject?"

The butler again examined the can of meat as if he had never seen it before.

"I'm sorry, Crocetta. It wasn't my decision, you know that."

"Which means your conscience is clear, I suppose. Anyway, I still have a week to spend here, and I'll still need to obey the guests, including the old soak from Emilia-Romagna. Like I said, he must have gone on a bender last night" – Crocetta tapped with her finger on the can – "and apparently, the doctor advised him to eat something very spicy to recover."

Bartolomeo nodded, still quiet and solemn. The things you have to do to survive. "All right. Just tell the gentleman he'll find it on the table."

"From what I understood, he'd like it in his room." Crocetta winked. "Seems to me he's ashamed to be seen with a hangover. He'll come down to the breakfast room later."

That's something at least, thought Bartolomeo.

~∞~

"Ladies and gentlemen, if I may have your attention, please."

Secondo Gazzolo looked at his guests gathered around the breakfast table.

"Today – may I say 'at last'? – we shall bid each other farewell. It wasn't the pleasant weekend we had all imagined, and what happened next, if possible, was even worse. But I think we will all listen with relief to the words Ispettore Saverio Maria Artistico is about to say to us."

After which, Hallelujah, we'll be free. Look what a state we're all in.

Among the guests, there wasn't one who didn't have red eyes. Red from weeping, like Delia's. Or red from lack of sleep, like those of Signor Viterbo, who had eaten rather less than usual, but apart from that seemed calm enough. Or red with anger like Bonci's – one red, actually, the other being purple. Best of all, red like those of Mantegazza and his friend Artusi, who had apparently polished off a whole bottle of brandy during the night. At least they had not been shut up in their rooms feeling desperate.

"Signor Gazzolo, ladies and gentlemen. A few words just to tell you that there is no reason for any of you to linger here any longer. It has been ascertained that the death of poor Signor

D'Ancona is to be ascribed to natural causes, and as far as the other events that occurred are concerned, nothing indicates the need for further on the spot investigations. I am sorry for any bother that I have caused with my presence, and I thank the master and mistress of the house for their hospitality."

A restless dragging of chairs greeted the inspector's words. The guests were like so many hundred-metre runners at table, each seated on the edge of his or her chair, one foot forward and the other behind as if on the starting blocks.

"You have done your duty, Ispettore. And now, ladies and gentlemen, I think Signor Aliyan also wishes to say a few words."

"Thank you, Gazzolo *effendi*. I should just like to say that I'm aware of how much the things that have happened have upset us all, but I should like you to understand that I was particularly close to Everardo D'Ancona, and that his death is particularly painful for me. That is why, in order to bid him farewell with dignity, I would like to ask a little favour."

Aliyan made the gesture of throwing something behind his back, to indicate a place distant in time and space.

"In the place where I was born, in the mountains of Anatolia, we have a custom. When someone dear to us dies, we release his favourite animal. So now, with the permission of the master of the house, I should like to go to the pigeon loft and release his pigeons, who will fly home, to Rome and to Milan, ready to serve whoever takes Signor D'Ancona's place in his work, even if never in our hearts. If any of you wish to follow me, that would give me immense pleasure."

"I think, Signor Aliyan, that for all of us it would be an honour to accompany you," Ispettore Artistico said in a solemn tone, looking around in an eloquent fashion.

Yes, of course we understand. Anything just to get out of here, as quickly as possible, any way we can.

Bright, diagonal shafts of light came in, bringing in their wake grains of dust that flew about, playing hide and seek.

Aliyan had solemnly tied red bands to the feet of the three pigeons while they were still in their cage. Then the cage was opened, in respectful silence, and one after the other, the birds were thrown by Aliyan through the window. After a few metres, with everyone watching them, they turned east, towards the rising sun.

All three of them.

After a few seconds, Viterbo said:

"Excuse me, but . . ."

"Go on, Signor Viterbo," the inspector said encouragingly. It seemed he needed encouragement: he was in jacket and tie, he was sweating a lot and was out of breath. Of course, it wasn't easy for anyone to get up to the pigeon loft, climbing a stepladder and squeezing through a narrow trapdoor. Some had managed it easily, others with difficulty, Signor Viterbo like toothpaste oozing out of a tube.

"I don't understand much about pigeons, but isn't Rome that way?" Viterbo said, pointing south.

"Indeed, Signor Viterbo. I can assure you that Rome is still where it was founded. South of here. Milan, on the other hand, is to the north."

"So why did the pigeons all go the same way?"

"Because the pigeons didn't go either to Rome or to Milan. They returned home, to the pigeon loft on the Campoventoso farm. Am I right, Signor Gazzolo?"

"I don't understand why you're asking me, Ispettore."

"Why? Because it was you who took care of Signor D'Ancona's pigeons every time he came and spent the night here. Which means it was you, every time, who replaced them."

The master of the house cleared his throat and said in an irritable tone:

"Ispettore, this is absurd. I don't think you understand enough about carrier pigeons. These birds do not travel in a straight line, nor do they head immediately for their destination. It takes them a few hundred metres before—"

"Ah, I see. So, if we now go to the other pigeon loft, we won't find three pigeons with red bands tied to their feet, is that right?"

All eyes turned to the master of the house. The inspector kept looking fixedly at him as he went on:

"Actually, no, Signor Gazzolo. We'll find four. Four, because there were four pigeons. One of them I myself released last night, at about four o'clock, together with Senator Mantegazza and Signor Artusi, having first attached to its foot a red bow and a piece of paper signed by all three of us."

The inspector continued looking harshly at the master of the house.

"Also last night, these two gentlemen and I went to the pigeon loft on the farm, which is less than a quarter of an hour's walk from here. And there we found the bird. The pigeon we had just released had easily found its way home. You who understand about pigeons, Signor Gazzolo, know perfectly well that these animals are able to fly even by night. And you know perfectly well that carrier pigeons always return home."

"Ispettore, excuse me, but why would my husband have replaced these pigeons?"

Signora Clara's voice sounded different – slightly shrill, but also quivery, a bit like lemon jelly.

"To create a double arrival point," the inspector replied, turning to her. "The pigeons that D'Ancona brought were replaced on his arrival with pigeons of the same species. In this way, when D'Ancona sent a message, it first reached the pigeon loft on the estate, which was the pigeon's arrival point, its home. Then once the letter had been read, it was put back, and the original pigeon, the one brought by Signor D'Ancona, could leave for Rome. Or Milan."

The inspector turned and once again addressed Gazzolo.

"That way the message arrived, and arrived quickly. It didn't take more than half an hour for the letter to be read and the pigeon replaced. Nobody in Rome or Milan would have noticed any delay. Just as nobody would have noticed that the message had been tampered with, because it hadn't been changed in any way, had it?"

"Variety."

"What?"

"You said that the pigeons were replaced with others of the same species. You should have said variety. All carrier pigeons are *Columba livia*, but mine are of the Antwerp variety. That was your first mistake. Your second mistake is that it wasn't I who attended to the pigeons but my butler. Your third mistake was when you said 'when D'Ancona sent'. You should have said 'if D'Ancona had sent'. Apart from that, you're right."

Gazzolo's voice remained calm.

"It was I who gave orders to Bartolomeo to change the pigeons, as I've always done, whenever Signor D'Ancona spent the weekend here. It was a simple precaution. In my line of work, it's always an inestimable advantage to have information that others don't have. It struck me that if Signor D'Ancona ever did use that means of communication, it could be useful to me."

"It's an offence, Signor Gazzolo."

"Only if I had committed it, Ispettore. But such an eventuality never arrived. You can check, if you want. During the times Signor D'Ancona stayed here, not a single letter reached Rome, or Milan, via pigeon post."

The inspector nodded, slowly. He seemed convinced. "Be that as it may, in the end, just before everyone was due to depart, Bartolomeo was again charged with replacing the pigeons."

"Precisely, Ispettore. He didn't do so in the last few days. He should have done it this morning, but someone had barred access to the pigeon loft, without having permission to do so." Secondo Gazzolo smiled amiably at the inspector. "Now I've understood why. If Bartolomeo had put the birds back in place, you wouldn't have been able to stage your little *coup de théâtre.*"

"You understand and don't understand, Signor Gazzolo. In reality, the purpose was subtly different. But in the meantime, let's try to conclude the matter of the pigeons. You gave orders to Bartolomeo to put back the missing pigeon?"

"What pigeon, excuse me? There were four pigeons. One you released last night, the other three you released this morning. 3 + 1 equals 4, unless the Italian government decides to change the rules of mathematics."

The possibility to which Gazzolo was referring was not as bizarre as it might seem. Only three years had passed since, in 1897, the senator for the state of Indiana, Taylor E. Record, had proposed legislation to change the value of pi, making it equal to 3.2 instead of the extremely complicated 3.141592, which would have simplified all calculations regarding circles. The proposal had been narrowly defeated. Of course, in dear old Europe, the law could not change a scientific fact: some things, it was thought then, could only happen in America.

"I mean the pigeon that Signor D'Ancona sent, and which was put back in its place after completing its brief flight and landing in the estate's pigeon loft last Saturday."

"Ispettore, perhaps I didn't make myself clear: Signor D'Ancona never sent any letter when he was here. If there were four pigeons and you found four . . ."

"Allow me, Signor Gazzolo. You see, I'm certain that D'Ancona came up here. I'm certain of it, because he knew perfectly well that the pigeons had been replaced. He told Signor Artusi about it. Am I right, Signor Artusi?"

Pellegrino Artusi nodded.

Not directly, of course. But he had given a fairly specific hint. No. 176. The little story in which an unpleasant gentleman arrives at a restaurant with some plump thrushes which he has marked by cutting off their tongues, these are exchanged, and the waiters cut the tongues off some similar but very thin birds. And the customer doesn't recognise the thrushes, because they are marked like his.

Signor D'Ancona had been unaware of this ploy until the day he had gone to the pigeon loft to actually send a message via pigeon – and wearing his new glasses, to boot. After seeing the pigeon set off in a somewhat unexpected direction, he had taken a closer look at the birds and realised that these pigeons weren't his.

"At this point, I ask you to follow my reasoning: Signor D'Ancona knew that his precious birds had been replaced, which means that he had gone to the pigeon loft." Artistico pointed to the stepladder up which everyone had ventured. "And you'd like me to believe that he wouldn't have sent anything? For what reason on earth would an elderly man of delicate health have tackled such a ladder if not to send a letter?"

The inspector opened his hands wide. Around him, spontaneously, a circle had formed.

"I'm reasonably sure that this letter, the missive in which he gave details of the fraud, and which he had previously hinted at in his telegram, was actually sent. So then the question is: what fraud? What fraud was he referring to?"

"Ispettore, unfortunately we know perfectly well what

fraud he was referring to," Viterbo said. "Let's try to move on, I beg you."

"You mean, Signor Bonci's insurance fraud?"

"It's not a fraud," Bonci tried to say, but Artistico froze him with a gesture of the hand, like an early-twentieth-century superhero.

"No, gentlemen, no. Think about it a moment. The trade licence had not been issued to Signor Bonci, it was still up to D'Ancona to decide on it, so why should D'Ancona have blocked with such urgency something that in reality was not yet in existence?"

"The contracts were ready, and the agreements had all been signed," ventured Aliyan, but it was clear that Artistico's argument had raised doubts in his mind. "But yes, there would have been no reason to alert the Chamber of Commerce. And besides, Signor D'Ancona trusted Signor Viterbo. He had no doubts about the solidity of Signor Bonci's proposal."

"You see? D'Ancona's behaviour would only have made sense if it had concerned a person who already had such a licence and was about to commit a massive fraud on the OPDA, the Ottoman Empire or both."

"Are you talking about me?" Gazzolo asked.

❧

"You are the only person who answers to that description, Signor Gazzolo."

"All right. Then explain to me what on earth this mysterious fraud of mine would have consisted of?"

"I could explain it to you, Signor Gazzolo. But it might be better if Signor Artusi does so, as he understands a lot more about these things than I do."

"Are you also a fraudster, Signor Artusi?" Gazzolo's voice was sarcastic, perhaps slightly too much so. "Then welcome to our little club. That makes three of us now, perhaps someone else would like to join."

Pellegrino Artusi shook his head. He was as red as a pepper, even though, given what he was about to say, someone else should have been blushing, not out of shyness but with shame.

"I'm sorry, Signor Gazzolo, I have been called many names, but I am not a fraudster. And I regret having to say these things in your house, since I am your guest, but I don't like your taking advantage of me."

Artusi took a deep breath, put his hands behind his back, looked through the window and started speaking.

"When you sent me some samples of your canned stewed meat, I found it too spicy for my taste and the meat struck me as ferrous and tough. Like beef that was too old or over-cooked."

"*De gustibus* . . ." Gazzolo said, stuffing his hands in his pockets. "I don't think I treated you with the same severity."

"You did worse. You tried to deceive me. You see, the question you asked me was: Is this a good product? And I answered that question. But last night Ispettore Artistico asked me another question. And having to answer a different question, I tasted it in a different way, and understood."

"And what question was it that you asked him, Ispettore?"

Signora Clara's tone was a real mistress-of-the-house tone, the kind that mistresses of the house adopt when someone says they have eaten better somewhere else.

"He asked me what kind of meat it was, signora. If I was sure it was beef, or if it could possibly be pork."

A brief silence. A hushed, disquieting silence. The kind that falls just after a bomb has gone off.

"Bartolomeo, hold the ladder for me," Signora Clara said after a moment. "I have no intention of staying here while insults are hurled at my—"

"Clara, please be quiet," said Gazzolo, calmly.

9

"The procedure is a simple one, Ispettore. First, you make a meat stock. You cook the meat in a mixture of cold water and herbs, in such a way that it stews and gives a fine tasty stock. The boiled meat, which is beef, is worked into balls that are then put in tomato sauce. They are canned and sold as meatballs in sauce and are intended exclusively for the Italian market."

Gazzolo rolled the cigar between his fingers – it had gone out sometime earlier – and placed it on the desk.

He had asked permission to continue the conversation in private: having his wife and, above all, Aliyan in the same room would have caused him quite a degree of embarrassment. Ispettore Artistico had consented but requested the presence of witnesses. He had agreed that the faithful Bartolomeo could be one of them and stipulated that on his side Pellegrino Artusi and Paolo Mantegazza should be present, although he asked them not to intervene unless they were specifically questioned.

"The stock obtained from this, with the addition of fresh beef blood, is used to cook pork using the vacuum-sealing technique. Thanks to this technique, the meat absorbs and incorporates the creatinine and myoglobin from the stock and, thanks to the blood, assumes the ferrous quality typical of beef. The addition of spices, which are particularly appreciated in some parts of the world, gives it an exotic touch and further increases the taste. This product is intended solely for the Ottoman army."

"And you're able to sell pork for the price of beef."

"Actually, a little less, or nobody would buy it."

"And to be absolutely on the safe side, you went into a market where nobody has ever tasted pork and so wouldn't be able to recognise it."

Gazzolo smiled. "Well, let me tell you, not even the greatest Italian gastronome recognised it."

That was indeed something to be proud of. Behind him, the inspector heard the person in question shift on his chair.

"So that was your intention when you visited Signor Artusi in Florence? You weren't looking for publicity, but putting your product to the test?"

"Well, I'd say I succeeded, wouldn't you? I could hardly have sold it as pork to the Ottoman army, could I?"

"You could have sold them actual beef."

"Not at a competitive price. It costs me too much. We're talking about a market of millions of people. Even five cents makes a huge difference. It's not easy to make food of quality if you're not prepared to spend money. We have here the greatest expert on these things, I'm sure he'll confirm that to you."

Ispettore Artistico turned. "Signor Artusi, do you have anything to say?"

"Signor Gazzolo, you flatter me unduly. I'm only a compiler. I write down and report on other people's recipes. I'm not a cook, and I don't claim to be one." Artusi put his hands together in front of his face (and, consequently, in front of his whiskers) and shook his head slowly. "You see, Signor Gazzolo, you were under the illusion that being the best-*known* expert on food, I was the best. That nobody could have a more discerning palate than mine. But clearly Signor D'Ancona was better than me. I don't know how he discovered you, but I am inclined to think that he tasted your product and spotted what I hadn't spotted at all."

"You are too hard on yourself, Signor Artusi," said the inspector. "Signor D'Ancona's palate was probably more accustomed than yours to spicy food."

The inspector was Calabrian and knew what he was talking about. During the first years of his posting to Tuscany, he had often wondered why in the Maremma they didn't put salt in bread or pepper in anything.

"Having gone back and forth between Italy and Turkey in the last few years, he had got used to spicy foods and they hadn't obliterated his ability for judgement, as happened to you."

"It's possible, you know," Mantegazza cut in. "D'Ancona asked me a curious question about that. He asked me if we lose our sense of taste as we age. Who knows if . . ."

"All right, Ispettore. You've caught me. Now if you'll forgive me, I have a business to run, so we need to be practical. At this point, my question is: What is my punishment likely to be?"

"That depends, Signor Gazzolo. It depends what crime we're talking about."

"That's just it. I'd like to be clear as to how you consider the matter. Technically, at the time of Signor D'Ancona's death, the contract hadn't been ratified, and obviously I'm ready to withdraw the product from the agreement with the Ottomans. In addition, even though up until now we have talked about fraud, you will agree with me that this wasn't fraud, merely deception."

The distinction between these two things was a subtle, but important one. You defraud someone when you sell him something that doesn't exist, duping the buyer and causing him financial harm; but you deceive him if, for example, you deliver to him something different from what was agreed, like pork sold at the price of pork, but making him believe that it is beef. There is cheating involved, but no harm is done, and it is a less serious offence.

Gazzolo's question was not inappropriate, but Ispettore Artistico shook his head. "No, Signor Gazzolo. I'm not talking about either fraud or deception. I'm talking about the murder of Signor Everardo D'Ancona."

"Ispettore, you said yourself that—"

"I lied. I needed to pacify you, or there would have been an almighty fuss."

Gazzolo's hand came down violently on the desk, with a noise like a chandelier. "You mean I'd be making an almighty fuss!" he said angrily. "What makes you so sure I killed Signor D'Ancona? To kill someone, you need a motive!"

"We touched on the motive just now, Signor Gazzolo. Your fraud – or your deception – had been discovered."

"Then you're an idiot. I didn't know he had discovered me, don't you see? *I didn't know.* How on earth did you come up with this nonsense?" Gazzolo's voice, which had gone up in volume, suddenly quietened down, turning low and calm. "You keep saying that Signor D'Ancona had realised that my product was made from pork. Well, you may say it, Ispettore, and forgive me if I got upset, but this is just a supposition of yours. Where does it come from, I'd like to know?"

"From the pigeon that was put back in its place."

"That pigeon again? But for what reason, for God's sake, should I have put that damned pigeon back in its place?"

"As a precaution. To prevent Signor D'Ancona discovering that a pigeon was missing. Thereby preventing a policeman arriving at great speed from Siena from being able to discover that in reality the famous letter that described the fraud had really been sent. Because that letter, as I was saying, was really sent. Just as it's true that Signor D'Ancona was really suffocated."

Secondo Gazzolo was now openly smiling. "Wait, wait, let's see. According to you, at some time in the night I turn into a disembodied spirit and get into Signor D'Ancona's locked room, choke him to death, then leave, after putting the draught excluder back behind the door, is that right? I'm not sure how I did it, but I'm sure you're about to explain it to me. All this while two people are talking to me and playing billiards in my presence all night long until five in the morning, when my manager and I set off on our inspection of the estate."

"Yes, that's more or less it. Only, nobody moved the draught excluder. It remained in its place throughout."

"You're insane. You tell him, Signor Artusi. Was I or was I not with you and Signor Viterbo all night?"

Both Gazzolo and Artistico turned to their key witness: Pellegrino Artusi from Forlimpopoli. He was as red as one of his beloved peppers. "Yes, Signor Gazzolo. That's right. We were together all night. But you see . . ."

"But you see, Signor Gazzolo, nobody says it was just you. You had help, an accomplice. The most sincere and loyal help you could hope for."

This time, Gazzolo did not turn. Behind him, Bartolomeo rose to his full height, like a Roman statue.

"If it may interest the inspector, I took my leave of the master and mistress about 10.30 and repaired to the kitchen for a game of cards." The butler coughed. "The game went on until the morning, when I went on duty. I was not alone until six in the morning. If I remember correctly, Professore Mantegazza declared that Signor D'Ancona had expired some hours before we found him."

"You won a good deal while playing, I hope."

"A satisfactory amount, sir."

"I'm pleased for you. But you see, Bartolomeo, your alibi isn't worth a fig," said the inspector harshly. "And neither is yours, Signor Gazzolo."

Secondo Gazzolo smiled. "Am I a magician then? Able to kill people with the force of my thoughts?"

Artistico stood up from his chair and started walking, his hands behind his back. "No, Signor Gazzolo. You're an efficient modern businessman, and, as you have shown, particularly well versed in chemistry. Please continue, Signor Artusi."

The inspector looked at him encouragingly, but Artusi shook his head.

"If you don't feel like it, Pellegrino, I can continue," proposed Professore Mantegazza.

"Yes, Professore, I'd be grateful."

"Last night, Signor Artusi told us that he had visited a curious place while on a journey to Naples more than fifty years ago. The place is a thermal grotto at Agnano, very close to Naples in fact, and is known as the Cave of Dogs. This strange name derives from the fact that some even stranger phenomena have occurred there. For example, a man standing inside the grotto can breathe normally, while a dog loses consciousness and dies soon afterwards. This is because of the carbonic acid, which makes the atmosphere unbreathable up to half a metre from the ground, or a little more. Carbonic acid is heavier than air and therefore stratifies at a low level."

A heavy atmosphere. That was the expression Ispettore Artistico had used, referring metaphorically to his own condition, and which had reawakened in Pellegrino Artusi's brain that memory from his long-ago travels.

"The same thing could happen in a bedroom: a person lying down with his nostrils and mouth half a metre from the floor would die, while people standing in the same room would suffer no ill effects and wouldn't even feel faint."

Secondo Gazzolo was now looking at Mantegazza as if hypnotised.

"This would explain all the evidence that has been presented. Signor D'Ancona's death by asphyxiation from an accumulation of carbon dioxide, and the faintness felt by Signorina Delia, who took refuge under the bed to avoid being discovered in someone else's room and found the atmosphere polluted, while you were able to enter the room a little earlier with no difficulty because your height placed you out of reach of any possible poisoning."

Gazzolo's usually impassive face was different now. His chin was quivering.

"Fortunately, time had passed, and the door of the room had been opened several times, a change in air which saved Signorina Delia. She doesn't know this, but she'd been in great danger."

Secondo Gazzolo reached his hand out for his cigar. But once he had taken it, instead of lighting it he crushed it in his fist. Then, with apparent calm, he began to rub his palm on the desk, to free it of the tobacco that had remained stuck to it.

"I assume you have proof to back up your absurd assertions," he said, still with apparent calm.

"Proof, you say. Could you ask your butler to take off his gloves?"

Secondo Gazzolo looked at Professore Mantegazza as if he no longer recognised him. "What's that got to do with anything?"

"Please, Signor Gazzolo. Either you ask him, or I'll take them off him myself."

Secondo Gazzolo turned to his butler. Who was usually also impassive if ruddy-faced. Right now, though, he was pale.

"Bartolomeo, take off your gloves."

The butler did as he was told, his hands shaking. Mantegazza went up to him and with professional delicacy turned his right-hand palm up. Then the left. On both palms there were large burns. Strange-looking, translucent burns.

"These are cold burns," Mantegazza said, in a diagnostic tone.

"Lesions typical of those who handle dry ice without appropriate protection."

Come on, this is too good to be true. So the butler did it?

~~~

"Dry ice is simply solid carbon dioxide. At temperatures higher than minus 78 degrees centigrade, dry ice sublimates, without passing through a liquid state, and turns directly into gas. To saturate a room like the one where Signor D'Ancona was sleeping – and bear in mind that the room only had to be filled up to a height of one metre – would take about ten cubic metres."

Nodding and slowly shaking his head, Secondo Gazzolo looked at his butler's hands, then at his own.

Ten cubic metres means 10,000 litres. In other words, since the molecular weight of carbon dioxide is 48 grams, about 20 kilos. Exactly the weight of a bucket filled with dry ice.

The same bucket that Gazzolo had entrusted to Bartolomeo on Saturday afternoon.

~~~

"The bucket was carried to the room, and your butler hid the dry ice between the logs in the fireplace. It started to sublimate immediately, but above one metre in height the gas had no effect. Then Signor D'Ancona came into the room and lay down on the bed, thus ensuring his death."

"You said it. My butler. Not me. You will have to explain, at this point, why you're also accusing me."

"Because it was you who gave the order to Bartolomeo to put the ice in the fireplace."

"There's no way you can prove that."

The butler had again risen to his full height. If anyone had had to point out the nobleman in the room, they would no doubt have chosen him. "I can prove it, sir."

Unsettled, Gazzolo turned to the butler. "It's my word against yours."

"Not really, sir. If the inspector would be so kind as to listen to me . . ."

"Go on, Bartolomeo."

"You see, Ispettore, it often happened before last year that the meats went from the factory to the kitchen still preserved in dry ice."

"And what happened last year?"

"There was an accident, sir. Two kitchen workers, after taking out the meat, had left the filled container in a corner. One of them had lost the ring he was wearing on his finger, and they bent over the container to look for it. Both fainted and were taken away just in time. We didn't know at first what had happened, it was Signor Gazzolo who worked it out later."

Yes. The accident. The day before, talking about a servant having been injured in one eye, Gazzolo had said, "It's very nearly the most serious accident that's occurred since I've been here." This other one must have been the most serious, obviously.

"After what happened, Signor Gazzolo added an item to the house rules, which said—"

"The house rules?"

"Absolutely, Ispettore. Inside the castle there are very strict rules, which the master himself instituted when he took possession. The staff are absolutely forbidden to handle dangerous chemicals inside the building. Even just bringing them in from outside is tantamount to a violation and warrants dismissal. That is true for caustic soda and for all the concentrated products used for cleaning, and since last year it's also been true for dry ice."

"And nobody contravenes this rule?"

"Nobody, sir."

"Not even your master?"

"Bartolomeo, be careful of what you're saying."

"If you mean Signor Gazzolo, not even he. Apart from last Saturday, when he came into the house and handed me the container in question. We were seen by several people, both during the tour and at the front door."

Bartolomeo looked Gazzolo in the eyes for the second time in his life. The first time had been the previous Saturday, at about five o'clock. Then he again addressed the inspector.

"I think you will agree with me that it would not have made any sense to contravene a strict internal rule in such an obvious way unless the purpose were of vital importance."

Having said this, Bartolomeo took a deep breath and lowered his chin to his chest.

He would have to wait until he was in prison to feel free for the first time in his life.

Epilogue

"Up to three years."

"What?"

"Up to three years' imprisonment."

"Three years? Are you sure?"

"Article 413 of the Penal Code. That's what the inspector told me. 'Your father,' he said, 'risks up to three years' imprisonment and a fine of more than 100 lire.'"

"How much more?"

"The code doesn't say, Papa."

Signor Bonci put his hands in his comb-over and bowed his head.

In terms of spending power, 100 lire in 1900 was equivalent to about 500 euros today. But if a fine of 500 euros was bearable, spending three years in prison . . .

"Could they fine me 10,000?"

"It depends on the verdict, Papa. I think it's very, very unlikely. The judge hasn't yet found you guilty, you know."

"But he's bound to. There's evidence, there's—"

"It may not even go to trial." Delia gently put her hands on those of her father. "Listen, Papa. I've talked to Signor Viterbo and apologised for my callous behaviour. He's a very good person."

"Yes, my child, that's why I wanted—"

"He's a very good person," Delia went on, knowing she was in a strong position, "and he told me he could withdraw the charges."

"Really?"

"He could withdraw the charges, provided you consent to the marriage. To my marriage with you know who."

"But . . . but . . . this is blackmail! Blackmail pure and simple! You . . . you're—"

"I'm your daughter, Papa. Who do you think I learned it from?"

~❦~

"So, Ispettore, how goes it with you?"

"Quite well, I should say, Professore Mantegazza. The case is solved, I've gathered sufficient evidence, I have a full confession of the murder. Yes, I should say quite well."

"So Secondo, too, has confessed?"

"Fully, yes."

Mantegazza shook his head. "You know, during our nocturnal excursion, I was already convinced you were thinking of Gazzolo, but not of Bartolomeo, too."

"The master of the house, you mean? But the master of the house doesn't get the rooms ready, Professore. He doesn't prepare the wood in the fireplace or advise putting a draught excluder under the door. Whereas a butler can do all that much more easily, and without attracting any attention. To each man his own role, Professore."

"Yes, indeed. Good old Bartolomeo, a murderer. And my friend Secondo . . ."

"Ah, yes."

There ensued another of those silences you get in a lift, while Mantegazza let his eyes rove along the building, on which the words AWARD-WINNING GAZZOLO COMPANY appeared in large letters.

"What about the company?"

"Ah, the company. What can I tell you, Professore?"

Mantegazza shook his head incredulously. "And so all this, this jewel of progress, will go to ruin. Do you think it's fair that one person's guilt should be paid for by more than a hundred people?"

"No, Professore, I don't think it's fair. Now I hope you understand why I feel so bad."

⁓⧫⁓

"May I?"

"Yes. Please, please, come in."

"Thank you. May I sit down?"

Crocetta nodded, looking at the chair and thinking: Let's hope it stands. But Signor Viterbo let his gaze wander around the room.

A novel by Verga on the night table. Good, the girl could read. And she had excellent taste. Having weighed up the chair, Corrado Viterbo walked over to the small iron bedstead. Crocetta remained standing.

"Please sit down. I don't like talking to people who are standing."

Crocetta sat down.

"This is your room, after all. I'm the intruder here."

"Not for much longer," Crocetta said.

"I know, Crocetta, I know. How old are you?"

"Twenty-two, sir."

Viterbo nodded. "The right age. You have your whole life in front of you."

"You say that as if it was bound to be a pleasant thing."

"Well, in your current position, I have to admit, no."

"It can't be a really good time for you either, from what I hear."

Viterbo nodded slowly. "Are you always so blunt?"

Crocetta didn't say anything. She might already have over-stepped the mark.

"Anyway, no, it isn't a good time. I made an unpardonable mistake in my work."

"Well, with all the money you have you'll be able to make up for it soon enough."

Viterbo put his hands together and placed them on his belly. "No, Crocetta, no. I fear I have lost the trust of my customers. You see, Crocetta, I'm a banker and a business intermediary. I sell trust. If nobody trusts me anymore, I have nothing more to sell."

"You still have your house."

"Of course. A beautiful house, spacious and empty. I deluded myself that I could fill it with life, with newness, and you know how that went. In short, whichever way you look at it, I've made myself a laughing stock."

Crocetta was silent. She couldn't help but agree with him.

"I've made myself such a laughing stock that the best thing I could do would be to move to the country and start again from scratch." His hands still joined, Signor Viterbo started to tap his thumbs together. "You're right about one thing, Crocetta: I have a lot of money. And do you know how I intend to use it?"

"I don't think that's any concern of mine, sir."

"Oh, but it is your concern. It's very much your concern. You see, I intend to move here. I intend to acquire Signor Gazzolo's estate and business." Corrado Viterbo made a Papal gesture with his hand, as if wishing to embrace everything around him. "It's a functioning business, it's sound and it's innovative. And the market is favourable. We could do great things, if we work hard. But I need someone I can trust. Someone who already knows the place well, who's intelligent, honest and doesn't mince words. And who doesn't hold back from telling me when things are going wrong. I don't need someone who thinks like me, I need a pain in the arse who stings me like a horsefly. And I need a young person. All characteristics that you have, Crocetta."

Crocetta looked at Signor Viterbo, her eyes wide open. She was used to hearing herself called a pain in the arse, but not to considering it a compliment. "You mean, you're letting me stay here?"

"I'm asking you to work for me, yes. To be my official liaison between the house and the business. Housekeeper, estate manager, right hand, call it what you want."

"But why me?"

Because you have intelligence and guts, thought Viterbo. Because you did the right thing even knowing that it would rebound on you. Because you are the child I never had, but if I had had one, I would have liked it to be like you.

Corrado Viterbo looked at Crocetta and opened his hands. "I've told you. And you know, too."

"Signor Viterbo, you do realise I'm a woman, don't you?"

"Excuse the vulgarity, Crocetta, but I couldn't give a damn. I want to run a business, not a public bath."

~᠕᠍ᢞ~

"So, Aliyan *effendi* . . ."

"So, Signor Artusi, we must say goodbye. But we shall see each other again. And soon, I hope. On the Bosphorus, perhaps, next time?"

"Alas, alas, I can't assure you of that."

"But you are still interested in trading in our textiles, I hope."

"I don't know, Signor Aliyan. I really don't know. You see, I'm quite advanced in years, and I don't know if, at my age . . ."

"How old are you, Signor Artusi? Forgive me for asking, but you strike me as being in excellent form."

"I was born in 1820, my dear Aliyan *effendi*. I'm eighty-something."

"And how do you manage to maintain yourself like that? Not only in the body, I mean. I know quite a few people who are ten years younger than you, who have studied, and are, as poor Signor D'Ancona would have said, a lot less clear-headed. You, on the other hand, are very clear-headed."

Artusi sighed and shook his head. "Studying has nothing to do with it, you know. Or rather, it does. If you don't read, if you don't make an effort, you stay where you are. But even studying the same thing all the time, well, in the long run I think it gets you befuddled."

"Bef . . . I don't know this word."

Artusi smiled. We never know our own language well enough, so imagine learning another language.

"If I'm not abusing your patience too much, I could explain it to you with a story."

Pellegrino Artusi put his hands behind his back, and, looking into the distance, started to tell the story.

"One day, an esteemed university professor came into the lecture theatre holding in his hand a large empty glass vase. Looking at those present, he asked: 'Gentlemen, is this vase full or empty?' The students cried in unison: 'It's empty.' Then the professor took a little bag full of stones from beneath the desk and emptied it into the vase until it was full to the brim. 'Now, gentlemen, is the vase full or empty?' The students cried: 'Now it's full.' Then the professor took another little bag, this time full of sand, and emptied it into the vase. 'Well, gentlemen, is this vase full or empty?' The students cried: 'Now it's really full, Professore.' Then the professor called to an assistant, who brought him a small cup of coffee. The professor emptied the coffee into the vase, watched it being soaked up by the sand, and said:

'Gentlemen, when you see that nothing more will go in your head, change what you put inside it. And when you see that, even when you change it, nothing more goes in . . .'"

Pellegrino Artusi opened his arms wide, miming resignation.

". . . then it's time for a nice cup of coffee."

Artusi shook his head.

"You see, Signor Aliyan, a few days ago I was asked if I see the glass half full or half empty."

"I know that saying, but I've never liked it," Aliyan said with a smile. "For me, the important thing is that one should be in a position to fill the glass, and to empty it."

"I've never liked it either. As if we were glasses. But you're right, if one has something to pour, what does it matter how much is already in there?"

Artusi beat his ample belly with his hands, while the wind ruffled his whiskers and hair. The former thick, the latter sparse, both white.

"But to fill it, it's again important to know what goes in. And for me, Signor Aliyan, at the point I've reached, right now it's time for a nice cup of coffee. I've realised in the last few days that I've spent a great deal of my life buying and selling, and I don't think I have any great desire to continue. There is still room, of course, but for other things, of which I have greater need."

Aliyan bowed his head briefly. "I understand you, Signor Artusi. Allow me then to pay homage to you with something of mine."

Aliyan held out to Artusi a piece of paper rolled into a cylinder. Artusi took it, also smiling.

"Is this what I think it is?"

"I think so, Signor Artusi."

From the diary of Pellegrino Artusi

Florence, 3 November, 1900
I have finally found time to transcribe here the recipe of the dish
with walnuts and pomegranate that Signor Aliyan was good
enough to write out for me; but I have to state in advance that,
having cooked it personally only once, I am not sure this is the
best procedure.

Muhammara
500 grams of nuts; 3 red peppers; pomegranate seeds, 1 cup;
1 medium-size onion; 2 large cups chicken stock; two spoonfuls
of oil; 2 level teaspoons of sugar; cinnamon, turmeric, nutmeg

According to taste, this dish can also be made replacing the
peppers with chicken, as is sometimes done in Turkey; in this
case it is no longer an intermediate course, but rather a meat
stew, and quite a substantial one, although not particularly easy
to digest. In this respect, the dish has two different names according to whether or not it contains chicken, being called *acem
yahnisi* if it has chicken and *muhammara* if it has peppers.
If ever I carry this recipe over into future editions of my book,
I fear I will have to find some easier names for it; not because
they are ridiculous terms, as culinary terms often are, whether
they come from France, like *oeufs sur le canapé*, or from Italy,
like *baccalà montebianco*. I think, however, that if I kept their
original names few people would be able to remember them,
and nobody would ever cook them again.

So put the walnuts to roast in a large frying pan until you can smell the pleasant aroma of roasted walnuts coming from the pan; but be careful to take them off immediately, because if you let them cook too much, they turn black, bitter and inedible. The first of these does not matter much, since there are many things in cooking that are dark in colour and truly delicious, most notably chocolate; but among burnt foods, fat foods like walnuts are among the most sickening. Therefore, wait for them to cool down and crush them in a mortar until they are reduced to a coarse mush.

Then chop the onion with a mincing knife and put it in the frying pan, until it loses colour and becomes almost transparent. At this point, throw in the chicken – which you will have previously rubbed in absorbent paper to dry it and coated in oil or butter – or the peppers peeled over a flame. If you have put in chicken, add stock.

Then put in the crushed nuts and the pomegranate juice, the sugar and the spices. Cover and cook on a very low heat for about an hour, stirring often so that the walnuts do not grow too attached to the bottom of the pot.

I wonder here if it might not be wise to add a little water so that the steam takes away some of the sharpness: it is true that the sharp taste of the pomegranate would replace it most excellently, but true also that the nuts are fat, and a dish that tastes only of nuts without the right counterweight of sharpness would be sickening. In short, each person must find the right balance, to his own taste. I have cooked this dish only on one occasion, but I sincerely encourage you to try it, because if well cooked, it will make you cut a dashing figure, and will pay you back with interest for all the effort it demands; but you have to remember that it is a complicated dish, with many spices to which we are not accustomed, and I think it is quite easy to make mistakes.

To end

As always, when one writes a historical novel, one ends up talking, more or less consciously, about what is happening now. There are several aspects of this book that present disquieting similarities with today's world; and the most curious thing is that I haven't needed to invent any of them. Many of the improbable things that you have read, dear reader, are true.

It is true that carrier pigeons were the quickest method for sending a piece of information at the beginning of the twentieth century: what is rather astonishing, though, is that, depending on the amount of information, they still are.

In September 2009, a race was organised between the South African telephone company Telkom SA and a pigeon called Winston, property of Unlimited IT. The race consisted of downloading as rapidly as possible 4 gigabytes of data from Howick to Hillcrest, some 80 kilometres away. Winston, equipped with a microSD card, took two hours, 6 minutes and 57 seconds to carry the data (including the time necessary to upload the data onto the card and download it onto the computer at its destination); by then, the amount downloaded through an ADSL line was still less than 4% of the total.

It is true that corks from bottles of champagne and sparkling wine are much more dangerous than we think: it is estimated that every year in the world the number of deaths caused by corks popping out of bottles is greater than the number of deaths caused by spider bites. I hope this doesn't encourage anyone to become teetotal: wine production is fundamental to the smooth functioning of the Italian economy, just as its consumption is often indispensable for one's own smooth functioning.

It is true that at the end of the nineteenth century the Ottoman Empire was heavily linked to European finance through the OPDA, the head of which was often an Italian. Should anyone wish to know more about how the inability to use loans brought about the collapse of one of the largest empires in history, the academic works of Giampaolo Conte are accessible to all, exhaustive and fully documented. Later, soon after the period of our story, the young Turks (the original ones) came on the scene and the largest nation in the empire started to flourish again.

Curiously, it is also true that the first military alliance between the Ottoman Empire and the Kingdom of Italy happened under the banner of canned meat. Ever since 1876, when canned meat was exported for the first time from one continent to the other, the Italians had been pioneers and experimenters in this kind of product. The first can of meat of an acceptable colour and taste saw the light in Italy in 1881, thanks to the genius of Pietro Sada, an enterprising Milanese gastronome who was constantly looking for new methods of preserving his much sought-after meat for a longer time. Before then, it was mainly the armies who used this kind of food, which had made its official debut in war in 1853, with canned beef prepared by the Lancia company for the soldiers of the Kingdom of Sardinia who were fighting in the Crimea in defence of the holy places, side by side with the Ottoman army.

Last but not least, Professore Paolo Mantegazza was a real person, a physiologist, a senator and the tireless author of books on the most disparate subjects – not all of them worthy of going into in depth. As a genuine disciple of positivism, Mantegazza had a blind trust in science and in its ability to solve the problems that preoccupied people at the beginning of the last century.

In several cases, this trust was well placed: he was the principal Italian populariser of the theories of Darwin – with whom he corresponded regularly – and his books on hygiene and on its importance in the prevention of disease were widely disseminated and probably contributed not a little to the development of cities at the beginning of the twentieth century. In other cases, his enthusiasm for new discoveries led him to exaggerate just a tad: for example, he extolled the miraculous virtues of cocaine, to the extent of recommending its use and free distribution to the workers of the less well-off classes. At other times, his enthusiasm led him to expound mad ideas, such as eugenics: on this subject he at least had the good taste to write a novel of semi-science fiction, *A Day in Madeira*, rather than a pseudoscientific treatise, as Cesare Lombroso had done a few years earlier with *Criminal Man*, displaying much greater intellectual dishonesty.

Where Lombroso, rejected by the academic community which derided his research, turned to the masses of the ignorant, ramming shocking but easily understood theories down their throats, Mantegazza, by his own admission, addressed scholars, people able to elaborate and criticise, not just to swallow everything. So, as we have seen, he was not always on the right side, and at least in one case propounded aberrant ideas: but, if I were to draw up a personal balance sheet of the erotic senator's contribution to the young Italian state, I would have to say that he did more good than harm. An equally positive judgement – and here there are fewer doubts – can be made about the contribution of his friend and reader, Pellegrino Artusi from Forlimpopoli.

More recipes from the kitchen of Pellegrino Artusi

Frittele di polenta alla Lodigiana
Polenta fritters, Lodigiani style

530 ml milk
100 grams cornmeal
Make a polenta, salting it to taste before removing from the flame. While the polenta is still hot, pour it onto your work surface and, using a table knife dipped in cold water, spread it out so it's a little less than half a finger thick. When the polenta has cooled off, cut the dough into disks of about 5 cm in diameter. Cut as many as you can, reshaping the dough as necessary, until you have about 32 disks. Pair the disks and lay a thick slice of Gruyere cheese between each pair so that you have 15–16 fritters. Now whisk two eggs, as they are needed to gild the fritters. Dip each fritter in the egg mixture and then in breadcrumbs. Fry them in lard or olive oil.

Serve hot as a side dish with a roast.

Totani in gratella
Grilled squid

Squid (*Loligo*) belong to the cephalopod class and are known on the Adriatic coast as "calamaretti". Since that sea produces them small yet meaty and delicious when deep-fried, they are judged by gourmets to be a superb dish. In comparison, the

Mediterranean produces a larger fish – I have seen squid that looked like they weighed 200–300 grams; these, though, are not as good as those of the Adriatic. These large squid, even cut into pieces, would be tough when fried, so they are better stuffed and cooked on a grill, or stewed if they are very large. This fish has inside it a flexible bony plate, which is simply a rudimentary shell and must be removed before stuffing.

Cut off the tentacles, which are the arms of the squid, leaving the sac and head, and chop the tentacles finely together with some parsley and a very small amount of garlic. Mix this with lots of breadcrumbs and stuff the mixture into the sac of the squid; to close the mouth of the sac, stick it with a toothpick, which will be removed later. Season with oil, salt and pepper and cook, as I mentioned earlier, on the grill.

Should you ever find yourself in Naples, do not miss paying a visit to the Aquarium in the gardens of the Villa Nazionale where, among the many zoological wonders on display, you will be delighted to observe this slender, elegant cephalopod swimming and darting about gracefully. You will also admire the speed and dexterity of the soles as they suddenly disappear into the sand, covering themselves with it, perhaps to hide from some enemy who pursues them.

Returning to squid, which is not the most easily digestible fish, but excellent all year round: after having removed the cuttlebone from the calamaretti and squeezed out their eyes, wash and dry them, flour them and fry them in oil. Be very careful not to overcook the calamaretti, which is easily done if you do not pay attention. Otherwise, they shrivel up and become even more indigestible. Season while hot with salt and pepper.

Risotto alla Milanese III
Risotto, Milanese style III

Here is another way of preparing Milanese-style risotto, but without the pretence of taking over from the great Milanese chefs, who are very creative and experienced with regards to this dish.

300 grams risotto rice
50 grams butter
¼ a medium onion
200 ml Marsala wine
A pinch of saffron

Finely chop the onion then cook in half the butter until brown. Add the risotto rice, cooking for a couple of minutes, then add the Marsala wine. Add hot water or broth and simmer until fully cooked. Add the rest of the butter along with the saffron dissolved in a bit of warm water. Finally add a handful of grated Parmesan.

This serves three people.

Fricassea
Fricassée

A fricassée can be made with breast or with another lean cut of milk heifer, lamb or chicken. Here we will use the first item, breast of heifer, as our example. The same quantities may be used for lamb or chicken as well.

500 grams breast of heifer
50 grams butter
2 teaspoons flour
200 ml hot (not boiling) water
1 bouquet garni
2 egg yolks
½ a lemon

Bone and chop the breast, retaining the bones. Melt half the butter in a saucepan, adding the flour and stirring until the mixture turns nut brown. Gradually add the water, then throw in the bouquet garni, which you can make by tying together strips of onion and carrot along with stalks of parsley, basil and celery. Leave out the leaves of the herbs and celery, which will disintegrate and spoil the appearance of the fricassée, which should be a distinctive, pleasing straw colour. Once the mixture comes to a boil, add the meat and the rest of the butter, then season with salt and white pepper, which is the flower of black pepper. Cover the saucepan with a sheet of parchment paper held in place by the pot lid, and simmer over a low heat. When the meat is two-thirds done, remove the bouquet garni. If fresh mushrooms are in season, you can improve the fricassée by adding between 100 and 150 grams of finely sliced mushrooms. Otherwise use a few of the dried variety.

When you are ready to serve, remove the saucepan from the flame and stir in the egg yolks, beaten with lemon juice, a little at a time.

If you are using chicken for your fricassée, cut the bird into pieces at the joints, discarding the head, neck and feet, then cook the dish as above.

A fricassée prepared in this manner is a wholesome and sophisticated dish that is especially appealing to people whose palates have not been ruined by intense flavours and spicy foods.

Crostini di capperi
Crostini canapés with capers

50 grams capers
30 grams raisins
2 tablespoons sugar
20 grams untrimmed prosciutto ham
20 grams candied fruit
20 grams pine nuts

Roughly chop the capers. Cut the pine nuts into three pieces and finely dice the prosciutto. Chop the candied fruit into small cubes.

In a small saucepan heat a heaped teaspoon of flour with the sugar. Once the mixture is beginning to turn a nut brown, add half a cup of water with a splash of vinegar in it. Let the mixture cook until smooth, then add the other ingredients into the saucepan and simmer for 10 minutes. Taste throughout the cooking time to make sure the mixture tastes sweet and strong (I have not given the exact amount of vinegar needed, because different vinegars are of differing strength). Lightly toast some bread, or fry it in olive oil, then top it with the still-warm mixture.

You can serve these canapés cold halfway through dinner, if you prefer, as an *entremet* to amuse your dining companions between courses. The best bread for this dish is the English kind baked in a mould.

Cosciotto di castrato arrosto
Roast leg of wether

Wether is in season from October to May; the short-legged variety with brownish-red meat is preferable. Roast leg of wether is a nutritious and tasty cut that is particularly recommended for anyone who has a tendency towards stoutness.

Before preparing this dish, let the meat mature for several days; the exact length of time will depend on the ambient temperature. Before skewering the meat on the spit, pound it well with a wooden mallet, then skin it and bone it, taking care not to tear the meat as much as possible. Then tie the meat to keep it all together. Set the spit over a high flame, with a dripping pan beneath, and when the meat is half done reduce the heat. Baste the meat regularly with the sauce from the pan and some skimmed broth. Once the meat is almost done, salt it. Make sure that the wether is neither dry nor undercooked, and serve with the juices alongside in a gravy boat.

Torta coi pinoli
Pine nut pie

These pine nut cakes are so popular that some pastry shops sell out rapidly. To the uninitiated, this cake may appear to have been invented by a professor from the Sorbonne. Here is my perfect re-creation of it.

500 ml milk
100 grams medium weight semolina (The amount of semolina is approximate – make sure to use enough so that the cake will come out firm)
50 grams pine nuts
10 grams butter
65 grams sugar
A pinch of salt
½ teaspoon vanilla extract
2 eggs

Chop or crush the pine nuts until they are half the size of a grain of rice.

Once the semolina has been cooked in the milk, add the other ingredients with the eggs coming last, and mix together quickly.

Make a shortcrust pastry dough, using:

200 grams flour
100 grams butter
100 grams sugar
1 egg (If the egg doesn't moisten the flour sufficiently,
add a few drops of white wine or Marsala)

Grease a baking pan large enough so that the cake won't be more than two fingers tall. Cover the bottom of the pan with a thin layer of the pastry dough, then pour in the pine nut filling. Use strips of the dough to make a criss-cross grid on top. Glaze the pastry with beaten egg yolk and bake. Let cool before serving sprinkled with icing sugar.

Biscotto da servirsi con lo zabione
Biscotto to be served with zabaglione

3 eggs, separated
90 grams icing sugar
Lemon zest
50 grams potato starch
20 grams flour

Whip the yolks and the sugar for about half an hour then add the lemon zest. Whip the whites until stiff, then fold them into the yolk and sugar mixture. Sift the flour and potato starch and fold gently into the batter so that it stays fluffy and airy. Grease a ring cake pan with butter and dust with flour and icing sugar, then pour in the batter. Bake immediately in an oven until cooked. Remove from the pan only once cooled and pour the *zabaglione* into the middle. Serve immediately.

This should serve five to six people.

Zabaglione
Also known as zabaione

2 eggs
150 ml marsala wine
50 grams sugar
Whisk the *zabaglione* constantly in a metal bowl over a low flame.

Acknowledgements

This book was first conceived as a critical commentary on Pellegrino Artusi's book of recipes, seen within the historical and cultural context of the time. I put the idea to Samantha, who after much deep thought, replied:

"What a drag."

I immediately switched to writing a novel. So my first thank you goes to her.

Particular thanks go to those who suggested books for me to read.

A well-deserved thank you in the first place to Albiera Antinori, who has long nourished my inspiration with her products, for having given me her father Piero's book *The Hills of Chianti*, from which I have plundered a number of amusing episodes.

A second, no less important thank you goes to the stranger I met on a train who recommended me to read *The Janissary Tree* by Jason Goodwin, an excellent mystery novel set in mid-nineteenth-century Turkey.

Well-deserved thanks also to my trusted group of private editors: Virgilio, Serena, Mimmo, Letizia, Massimo, and the newcomer Virginia – who is owed an apology, because we arranged the editors' dinner to discuss the book before she had read it: we won't do that again – the ever-reliable Davide from Olmo Marmorito and Serena from Naples, who also gets the prize for the best birthday song of all time, and the Cheli & D'Elia duo who took part less than usual, having something much more important to deal with in the shape of a baby.

Last but not least, thank you to everyone at my publisher and in particular to Floriana, who saw the book through its finishing stages in conditions it would be an understatement to describe as uncomfortable – the proofs were prepared in mid-March 2020, I think the date alone should be a clue . . .

And, as always, my most heartfelt thank you goes to Samantha: in this way she appears at the beginning and end of the acknowledgements, and always at the centre of whatever I write.

MARCO MALVALDI was born in Pisa in 1974, and is both a crime novelist and a chemist. He is best known for his Bar Lume series set on the Tuscan Coast, and also for *The Art of Killing Well*, the first of his mystery series about Italian gastronome Pellegrino Artusi, for which he was awarded both the Isola d'Elba Award and the Castiglioncello Prize.

HOWARD CURTIS is a translator from Italian, French and Spanish. He has won several awards, and his translations were twice nominated for the *Independent* Foreign Fiction Prize.